PERIL IN PARADISE

PERIL IN PARADISE

A KAY FRANCIS MYSTERY

B.C. STONE

PERIL IN PARADISE

Copyright ©2014 by B. C. Stone
Albuquerque, NM
http://vagrantmoodwp.wordpress.com

Trouble in Paradise (motion picture) ©1932, Paramount Pictures. Screenplay by Samson Raphaelson. Adaption by Grover Jones. Based on the play *A Becsületes Megtaláló* (*The Honest Finder*) by Aladár László

Cover design © by B. C. Stone

Library of Congress Cataloging-in-Publication data
Stone, B.C.
Peril in paradise : a Kay Francis mystery / B.C. Stone. – 1st ed.
Summary : Strange things happening on the set of *Trouble in Paradise*, Kay Francis's latest prestige production for Paramount Pictures. There's been a murder and the victim is close, too close to her, and she fears she may be next. She enlists the aid of her old friend and favorite leading man William Powell to help her solve the baffling murder. Cameos include director Ernst Lubitsch and co-stars Herbert Marshall and Miriam Hopkins.
1. Francis, Kay, 1899-1968 – Fiction. 2. Paramount Pictures – Fiction.
3. William Powell, 1892-1984 – Fiction. 4. Motion picture actors and actresses – Fiction. 5. Detective and mystery stories – Fiction. 6. Trouble in Paradise (Motion picture) – Fiction. 6. Motion picture industry – California – Los Angeles – Fiction. 7. Hollywood (Los Angeles, Calif.) – Fiction. 8. Nineteen thirty- two, A.D. – Fiction. 9. Nineteen thirties – Fiction. I. Title.
PS3569.T6418.P547 2014   813.54—dc21

FIRST EDITION

Printed in the United States of America
10 9 8 7 6 5 4 3 2 1

CHAPTER 1 : MOONLIGHT AND CHAMPAGNE
(WIVES & LOVERS DON'T MIX)

"Do you see that moon, waiter? I want to see that moon in the champagne." Marshall floated the words with a languorous wistfulness.

"Yes, Baron. Moon in champagne."

"I want to see …"

"Yes?"

"And as for you, waiter – I don't want to see you at all."

A shroud of silence uneasily crept through the set, but only for a moment, then:

"CUT! PRINT IT! Great job. Now let's take fifteen minutes." Lubitsch got up from his director's chair and began to examine some notes. Around him was the usual rustling of bodies and equipment while a small group of staff milled about sharing some small talk.

Sipping her glass of tonic water, Kay Francis leaned on a nearby counter and smiled approvingly as she looked on in Herbert Marshall's direction. He was talking with two members of the technical staff when she caught his eye. He smiled at her, nodded, then excused himself and sauntered over in her direction, sporting his familiar, elegantly impish grin. As she gazed at him she wondered how anyone so polished could look so mischievous. Oh, well, it suited the character he was playing.

She beamed a wide smile as she walked up to Marshall. "Bravo, Herbert, marvelous work. I've a feeling about this film. I think it's going to turn out to be something special."

"Thank you, my dear," he said as he clasped her hand and gave it a delicate kiss. "Your blessing is important to me. Yes, I'm rather enjoying playing this Baron fellow, or whoever he is. A lot of things I can do with this story, and character." Marshall's velvety baritone voice, coated with his trademark drawing room British accent, flowed like virgin olive oil on hot panini, and provided the defining touch to his suave, über-urbane persona.

"I'm so envious," she interjected. "I don't have a thing to do 'till the second act. Miriam gets all those sexy opening scenes." Her voice purred with a touch of false whining.

"Ah, yes, my dear. But remember what the man said: they also serve who only stand and wait."

"But the man didn't tell us we could go stir crazy sitting around waiting and doing nothing." She tilted her head, raised her eyebrows slightly, flashed a modest smile and said softly, "By the way, do we still have our rendezvous tonight at my place, nine o'clock?"

Marshall frowned. "Sorry, my sweet. I ask your forgiveness, as I must break our engagement, with the greatest reluctance, I assure you. You see, my wife is arriving on the late train from Chicago, and if she ever found out about our – well, you realize she's not the understanding type. My … friendship of a couple years ago with, you know the lady, all but sent her over the edge."

"I won't pretend I'm not disappointed." She tossed her head and flashed one of her knowing smiles. "But you can't fool me."

"How's that, my dear?"

"Herbert darling, I've a confession to make to you."

"And what confession is that?"

"That you like me, in fact, you're just mad about me." Marshall smiled and nodded while she continued, "You can't deny it, especially after our private dinner the other night over at *Pierre's*, and where it led afterwards?"

A pensive look away from Marshall. "*Pierre's*. Ah yes. I do remember. But I disagree with that reviewer from the *Gazette*. The food there was adequate but to call it a great restaurant is positively ridiculous."

She smiled, even more coquettish, "Herbert, darling, you think of a food critic's silly review instead of us?"

Marshall gently took hold of her hand. "Of course I think of us, my sweet. I remember the lamp, I remember the night table, and I remember the night. But most of all, my dearest Kay, I remember you, and shall treasure our time together always. It was glorious, divine, wonderful. But – one must defer to marital propriety. At least when the wife is in town. And besides, tomorrow morning, when you awake out of your deliciously wonderful dream, and hear a knock, and the door opens, it'll be a maid serving you breakfast and not a jealous wife holding a revolver. And you'll be glad."

A long breath. "If you say so."

"I must say so, my dearest, and with a most heavy heart."

CHAPTER 2 : JEALOUSY IN PARADISE

Kay shook off her disappointment. After all, compensations were in the offing. She thought of her lunchtime tryst tomorrow with the screenwriter she'd taken a shine to. There was also that up-and-coming supporting actor who'd been attentive lately. She was still making up her mind about him, about both actually.

More important, she had other concerns, especially some artistic matters, to talk over with the great man. She began to walk back to Lubitsch's office. The long corridor was abuzz with people scurrying everywhere: secretaries and starlets decked out in nice dresses and wearing too much makeup, sharply attired young men carrying clipboards and walking in a hurry, older, overweight men in three piece suits chomping on cigars who wanted to look important and be acknowledged as producers, assistant producers or something. There was also the occasional rumpled looking type of middle years: distracted, unshaven, with ashy, charred face and baggy eyes as though he'd stayed awake all night. The attire was mothball-scented tweed jacket and flannel pants. She recognized him straight away. Everything about him spelled writer.

She found herself just outside Lubitsch's office, but hesitated before she knocked at the door as she heard voices inside. She recognized them at once as Miriam Hopkins' and the director's. She could always pick out Lubitsch's Central European twang, and Miriam's fingernails-on-the-blackboard screeching was unmistakable. She sneaked to a place beside the door, close enough to peek through the side window and hear the contents of the lively conversation.

Miriam was in a fancy dressing gown, her trademark frowsy blond curls in disarray as if she'd strode straight from her dressing room to Lubitsch's office. Lubitsch was in typical director's attire: stylish slacks and an expensive sweater. Kay experienced a little frisson as she admired his slim physique and roguish good looks.

Miriam spewed out her words rapid-fire. "Quit stalling; you're not fooling anyone. I just found out. You've got a nerve, paying that tall, skinny clotheshorse more than me. Four thousand dollars a week, more than double what I'm getting! What's she got that I haven't got?" She folded her arms and paced a few steps back and forth "And another thing – "

Lubitsch remained calm as he delivered his words slowly, carefully. "Now Miriam, darling, you know I've nothing to do with salaries." He emphasized the word darling with a slow, Old World accent while pronouncing it as 'dahling'.

"Don't give me that. You've got plenty of pull here,

I know it. Anyway, money's just the half of it. She gets all the juicy lines." A mild chuckle, then, "If she can pronounce them."

"Very catty, Miriam, even for you."

She ignored his reply and continued, "And in the second act you practically cut me out altogether."

"That's not exactly true, Miriam; you have scenes in the act."

"Don't try to mollify me. You bought her for four grand. Well, you can have me for nothing, because I QUIT! *Finis. Das Ende. Capiche*?" Her pallor had become noticeably more crimson.

As Miriam paused to gulp in a few breaths of air Lubitsch promptly seized the conversational vacuum. "My dear Miriam, calm down, and let me explain."

"Explain? What's there to explain? I'm through with this film, I just told you."

"Miriam, dearest. You're also forgetting about *Design for Living*, which we begin in a couple of months. That's such a showcase for you, the role of a lifetime. And such co-stars, Gary Cooper and Fredric March."

"Don't try to change the subject. It's this film I'm talking about."

"Very well, and as I was saying, you get top billing in *Trouble in Paradise*. We promised that and we delivered. And I must differ in your assessment; you upstage her from the beginning. Your entrance in the first scene with the Baron in that gold lamé dress, and all the spicy dialog. Pure poetry. There's a full twenty minutes before Kay is even on-screen."

Miriam smiled and her facial features softened. "Yes, it is rather a good scene isn't it?" A pause and a look away. "But you can't sweet talk your way out of this. The fact is she's still making more money than me, a lot more, and she has the best love scenes. You make it look like the Herbert Marshall character is really in love with her, not me."

"Now Miriam, dearest, I assure you – "

"You and your assurances. What good are they?" In ever louder voice she said: "I'll stay in your silly picture but let me tell you now: that ... playgirl's not going to steal this movie from me. I'll do whatever I have to do, but she's not going to make me second fiddle."

Lubitsch had been looking down at some papers on his desk. Then he glanced up. "Um. How's that, Miriam?"

"I said so help me I'll break her neck if I have to!"

She bolted out of the room, the door slamming behind her, all the while Kay discreetly hiding in the shadows.

CHAPTER 3 : MAID'S NIGHT OFF

The dream was so real. Maybe it was, since some of her in-the-flesh encounters, the good ones anyway, were more like dreams, or fantasies, just better. But this sensory montage emerged from the land of night, and all the same she luxuriated in her companion's attentions.

Mumbling in her half awake state, she whispered: *I'm not a movie star now, just a woman. So treat me as a woman. Take me, take me as you'd take any woman!*

She felt herself creeping near the edge, about to fall into oblivion and release into rapture and go … somewhere. She began to tremble and her breathing became faster.

But – what was that? A sound, a thud, something falling. And a faint voice in the distance. She wanted so to return to the reverie's comforting embrace and its longed for moment of deliverance. But more thuds, or were they pounds? Then a knocking at the door.

"Senorita Francis!"

No, not now. She rustled slowly, reluctantly, then sat

up, shook her head back and forth and wiped sleep from her eyes. As her hand brushed her hair back she felt moisture on her forehead. Then a deep sigh. "Yes, Lupe?"

"So sorry disturb you. Breakfast ready."

A long breath. She glanced at the clock. Six-thirty, right on time. "Yes, so it is. Bring it in." Her tired voice betrayed a conspicuous lack of enthusiasm.

She dutifully completed the meal, got up, put on her robe and wandered around, trying to get motivated for another day's shoot. But a more pleasant thought crept into her psyche. "Lupe," she called.

"Yes ma'am," Lupe said upon entering the room.

"I wanted to tell you, before I get ready and leave: things will be a little different tonight."

"Different, miss?"

"Yes. Tonight at this house I'll present the most splendiferous supper, catered by *Etienne's*, mind you."

"Yes ma'am."

Kay looked away a moment and let out a sigh. "Yes, the meal will mark the start of ... well, beginnings are always difficult and uncertain. We must put our best foot forward."

"Yes, ma'am."

"It will be a marvelous supper, but what's more important is the delivery. It must all be presented with a certain panache."

"Yes, miss."

She looked though the window and said, "Do you see the sunrise, Lupe?"

"Yes, ma'am."

"Well, this evening I want to see the sunset's soft glow blend with the twilight into an incandescent sheen that embraces the dinner table, and all of the dining room."

"Very good, miss."

"Speaking of presentation, the caterers will not be staying around."

Lupe smiled broadly as if in anticipation. "Then you are saying you need my assistance, ma'am?"

A rapid shake of the head in the negative. "Not at all, Lupe. So sweet of you to ask but you may have the night off." Her eyes brightened and she cooed, "The next morning too. Show up around … noon."

Lupe's smile vanished and she sufficed with a bland, "Thank you, ma'am. Most kind."

.

CHAPTER 4 : TENSION AT BARKIE'S DINER

Cigarette smoke loomed heavy in the dimly lit cafe while a popular tune wafted from an indeterminate source. The snappily dressed couple at the far corner booth were nestled amidst a collection of nondescript customers who paid them no attention, busy as they were nursing coffee, munching their hamburgers and reading the papers.

After all the girl was just another ingénue in a city filled with such creatures and the man who sat across from her was better known for his name which appeared above the marquee of pictures. Otherwise his features were unknown.

The girl delivered her words in a loud, fast voice. "You keep pawning me off to the B department and they give me these awful little roles. And those weird odd jobs. I'm supposed to be a real actress, not a waitress or errand girl. You promised me much more of a career, and faster."

Her unlikely companion listened and nodded,

slowly, sympathetically. But his thoughts were elsewhere. No character in his films was anything like this, none quite so malevolent or spiteful. Being with this woman, whether in the bedroom or a restaurant, was not the usual sensual frolic but more like a struggle, a kind of exquisitely pleasurable agony in which he descended into an abyss from which he didn't know if he'd ever return. This was the femme fatale from hell and he'd have to tread lightly.

"My dear Margaret – "

The woman snapped, "You know I don't like that name. Another thing. I won't be a sycophant for a mediocre actress whose career is going nowhere. Sending me out for coffee. What kind of work is that for a real actress? That … prima donna is the most pampered woman in the studio and I won't be one of her servants."

As she spoke he noticed her curious hand gestures and elaborate facial and speaking mannerisms which seemed to him a collection of celebrity tics she picked up by perusing movie glamour magazines and taking in too many B movies with too many B actresses.

The man affected a smile that said patience but hinted of something else. "If you insist, my dear."

"I insist."

"As you wish." A deep breath. "We've been through all this before. As you suggest, I implied a lot, and I've been patient with you, bringing you along slowly. But now I must ask the same in return. A star's career doesn't take off overnight, my sweet. Remember, I'm in a position where I can do a lot of good for you."

"Seems I've heard that one before." Her voice became louder and she raised her arms, palms open in melodramatic fashion. "Oh, yes, I promise you the world, millions, fame. But for now just give me your ass." She paused and had a look around. "By the way, charming place, you make a girl feel real special."

The man glanced conspiratorially at the other customers and spoke in a tone that was more a hiss, his thick German accent coming to the fore. "Not so loud. Get hold of yourself. You'll call attention to us."

"Let them look. And listen. I'm going to start yelling any minute!"

He held up the palm of his right hand in a soothing gesture. "Just calm down."

"You're the one who'd better calm down. Remember, Ernst," she said, pronouncing her words softer, slower. "There are people who'd find it very interesting to learn about our, shall we say, special arrangement of mentor and protégé. The gossips, for instance? Maybe I'll just publish it all in the *The Tatler*. My early memoirs. What do you think?"

He glanced away, beads of sweat and tight lines appearing on his forehead. The next words he spoke he pronounced his words with a malevolent deliberateness. "My dear Leenushka. It's not nice to threaten, especially someone in a position to ... help you."

"It sounds like you're the one doing the threatening, dear Ernst, or is it Herr Direktor, or just Der Führer? It must be time for you to give me the old I-have-to-take-measures-with-you speech." She slammed down her soda on the table. "You're disgusting. Thanks for the elegant dinner." She bounded up and stormed out of the restaurant. She didn't look back.

B. C. STONE

CHAPTER 5 : A SECRETARY
BY ANY OTHER NAME

Immersed in one another, she and her companion lounged on the large sofa.

"My dear René, you simply take the breath away. By the way, is that your real name?" She waved a hand in a gesture of dismissal. "Oh, it doesn't matter; you're such good company. Your name, by any other name … What's that phrase anyway? I get it mixed up, all this literary stuff."

"A rose by any other name would smell as sweet. An apt quote for present company."

She clasped his hand and gave it a delicate kiss. "You say the nicest things, and I just love the sound of your voice, so smooth, masculine, flowing like thick warm brandy."

"Thank you, my dearest Kay. By the way, splendid dinner. You outdid yourself; you spoil me something awful. It almost makes me happy to be one of the nouveau poor: all the extra time on one's hands, not worrying about getting to bed and arising tomorrow morning and all that."

As she glanced toward the bedroom, her companion continued. "But really, my darling. So much bother. And expense. Much as I appreciate the gesture, *Etienne's* is notorious for overcharging their clients. Indeed the restaurant's questionable practices are quite well known among the smart set."

"I hadn't heard that. My secretary usually takes care of these things, but she walked out on me a few days ago. The nerve. She thought I was too strict. And I thought I was too lax. Anyhow I had to tend to the details myself."

"A decided but understandable oversight in view of your circumstances. But I implore you. In times like these, one must exercise caution, restraint. Were I your business manager, or your father, both of which happily I'm not, I'd plain take you over my knee and proceed to give you a good spanking. In a moderated, businesslike way of course."

"Of course." She glanced at him and gave a hint of a smile. "Well, what would you do to me if you were, say, my secretary."

"The same, absolutely."

"You're hired."

CHAPTER 6 : PROWLING IN THE DARK

Waiting, waiting, waiting. Why did I take this harebrained job? Stupid. These kinds of operations were way too risky. She could go to USC next fall. Somehow we'd find the cash. But a job's a job, and I said I'd do it.

So wait he did, impatient and cranky in the cold night air, hoping against hope that his DeSoto Coupé would look inconspicuous in the narrow little street which ran through the studio's back lot.

He knew this was the exit she would take, and as far as he could tell no one had paid him any notice. The evening darkness and lateness of the hour had been allies. But there were drawbacks as well. The place was one of those thin streets which hugged the buildings, and a big car like his stood out.

But tonight a break: the evening fog which hung heavy in its spectral embrace of the studio property, the clouds and moisture lurking like a dense, pillowy carpet of fear. This was his best ally, the mist which cloaked

the block-long, barracks-like Paramount structures in its
wraithlike blanket. Definite images and shapes became
lost in gossamer drapery, the lamps reduced to
pinpricks of smeared light and his imposing car a soft,
dark blob.

He glanced and strained to get a glimpse of
something. He felt tired and his muscles ached; he
wasn't getting any younger, he often told himself. But
he also knew the hefty advance felt nice and tidy in his
coat pocket snuggling against his chest.

He took a drag on his Camel to calm his nerves. As
the smoke went down he let out a scratchy, lengthy
cough. Damn smoker's rasp. Not good. He didn't need
any extra noise right now.

Operations like these weren't anything new. But this
one was different, and not only because the mark was
sympathetic, and a woman at that. He'd done some
rough work in the past and it usually had something to
do with the studio, and he suspected as much this time.
The where and the when of this assignment pretty
much gave it away. He surmised the higher ups were
probably behind this one, whatever their reasons.

But he couldn't be sure. His employer never
communicated with him directly, but rather did
everything by telegram and phone calls, all heavily
coded. Even the voice was disguised. He couldn't tell if
he was dealing with a man or a woman. His instructions
were just do the job, no questions, and he'd get paid.
And when the pay was good he didn't ask questions.

He kept staring ahead but still there was the fog,
blending in with the night into a swamp of powdery
greys. Little wonder that the thoughts, and the
impatience, became more insistent with the passing

minutes.

He watched, but he also listened. The smallest sounds seeped through the dense forest of darkness and semi-darkness, magnified, teasing and threatening. He expected to catch a glimpse of her or hear the footsteps any minute. The sound of walking had a personality of its own – the weight, gait, pacing, type of shoe. He would recognize those sounds as he'd heard them before on dry run stakeouts.

Then the tap, tap, tap – a woman's walk, quick, decisive. A figure emerged from the blanket of fog, at first only a shadow of grey and black, but gradually more distinct. Yes, it was her all right: the stylish clothes, wide brimmed pull down hat, languorous stride and tall, svelte frame. He turned on the ignition switch and the large vehicle gurgled and rumbled like an impatient beast stalking its dinner.

The car began to move, slowly, ponderously, following the figure as she walked on the sidewalk paralleling the street. In a lurch his foot laid heavily on the pedal and then a burst of speed. A quick veer to the right. The tires jumped up onto the sidewalk and the woman turned round and let out a wild, screeching sound, a primeval shriek from the netherworld. Then a thud …

CHAPTER 7 : THE POLICE ARRIVE

The curtain of fog was lifting. A few gossamer strands remained and blended in with the tall man's cigarette smoke. He walked unsmiling toward his stocky colleague who'd just arrived.

"Hello, Fallon."

"What's doin', Archer?"

"Fun to be dragged out of bed again."

"Sure. A gas."

"You're tellin' me. Juanita and I were just starting to hum. I hadn't seen her in two weeks." He took a drag on his cigarette and looked away. "God, she's got a great body … then the damn phone rings."

"A tough break."

The men paced a few steps as they examined the general area. Both seemed reluctant to look down at the covered figure below. "Sure looks like hit and run," Fallon said. "A security guard found her a couple hours ago. Coroner and crime lab boys should be here pretty soon."

Archer nodded as he continued to look around. "Anybody see or hear anything?"

Fallon's eyes scanned upward. "Somebody must have, even in this pea soup fog. A big car like that makes noise. My guess is it was a DeSoto or Cadillac, maybe a Packard." He pointed down at the sidewalk. "See the tire tracks? They turned, just about … here, and jumped up on the sidewalk. Ten'll get you twenty the guy was aiming at her. And check this: the tire patterns. He backed up the car, then ran over her just to make sure."

"Nice guy. A professional?"

"It's likely. I had a look see at the body before you got here. The girl was a real beauty. And a sharp dresser. Probably an actress here."

"Yeah. But these studios are like fortresses. They lock 'em up real tight. Inside job?"

"Could be. The strangest thing, though."

"What's that?"

"We found this empty champagne bottle right beside her body."

Fallon handed the bottle to Archer, who examined it with a skeptical look. "*Beau Soir.* Never heard of it. Does it mean anything?"

"Hard to say. It's an expensive brand. So what's it doing here? A plant? Was it already here? Was the killer driving drunk? Things like this don't just fall out of cars by themselves. Looks like someone wanted to leave it."

"Strange calling card."

"Whatever. I doubt the bottle will tell any stories after they dust for prints and whatnot."

His partner looked at him and gave a nod in the opposite direction. "Uh-oh. Here comes trouble."

A grim-faced man strode up to them, hand outstretched. "Frank Lugg, deputy head of Paramount security."

After eyeing him warily, the two cops grudgingly shook his hand. Lugg was beefy and athletic, and had a sharp-edged, Lon Chaney face that revealed creeping lines of tension and fatigue.

"Do you recognize the girl?" Fallon said.

"Yeah, a B actress just starting out. Name's Leena Sparkle." He looked down at the body, shook his head and said in a tired, raspy voice, "Sad. Damn, the studio hates this kind of thing."

"You're all heart," Archer said.

"Take it easy," Lugg growled. "I'm just sayin' – "

"Never mind," Fallon said. "Can you get her bio and other important stuff to us?"

"Sure. You got it."

"Thanks."

B. C. STONE

CHAPTER 8 : BREAKFAST WITH
A TWIST OF MURDER

The early morning salt-scented mist crept up the hills and bathed the Bel Air property in a bright haze of soft evanescence. The estate's picturesque setting had an especially quiet, benign quality that day.

Gordon and Liddy Shellhammer sat at the patio table perusing the morning papers as they finished up breakfast's final scraps. Nursing some strong coffee as he read, Shellhammer glanced at the *Times* while Liddy favored the *Journal*.

"By the way," he said. "What happened to you last night over at Beaumont's? You just downright disappeared around midnight. Did you come back here?"

"Of course. Couldn't you tell I was irritated?"

"How could I tell? I was talking to the company, mingling, that sort of thing. You know how you're always telling me I need to be more civilized."

"Oh, come on. You know better than to give me that. I'll tell you what you were doing."

"What's that?"

"Talking to the crimson dress, that's what. You think I didn't notice? You practically monopolized her the whole evening. But I admire your taste. Nice curves."

A smile. "Did I monopolize her? Hmmm … Where did the time go? Well, perhaps you're right. All in a day's work"

"Gordon, what's your job again exactly?"

He drew in a deep breath and let it out slowly. "I'm special assistant to Mr. Janis, the executive director, which means my responsibilities are … flexible, and shall we say, situational."

"That's perfectly clear to me. Anyway it explains all the parties and ogling the young things. How's the steak and eggs?"

"Just great. Flossie outdid herself."

She took a sip of coffee, looked toward his paper and made a vague gesture with her hand. "What do you think of that?"

He affected a bemused stare. "That?"

"Yes. Right here." She pointed to a headline below the fold. "Wake up, man."

STARLET FOUND MURDERED. HIT AND RUN. POLICE STILL BAFFLED. The brutally crushed body of ingénue actress Leena Sparkle was found last night on Lot 3 of Paramount Studios, the young woman apparently the victim of a hit and run driver. Miss Sparkle was a rising star in the film industry. Authorities said this most hideous murder has the police stymied. The victim had no enemies, there is no apparent motive, and no suspects at this point have been identified. A spokesman for the studio said Miss Sparkle was a burgeoning talent with a bright future and that she will be greatly missed by all, also that everyone associated with the studio was cooperating fully with the police.

"I don't know what to think of it," he said. "By the way, aren't all murders hideous? Right." A thoughtful frown, then: "Yes, I know all about that. The security folks at the studio called me, the middle of the night call. Hope it didn't disturb you."

"Not at all, I didn't hear a thing. Just slept like a babe."

He managed an indulgent smile. "I've got to get on it first thing this morning. They're such sticklers about public relations, which reminds me I better be taking off. Sorry to leave so fast."

"Oh, it's okay. I'm used to it by now."

"You're a dear, truly the patience of a saint."

"Don't overdo it. You knew the girl?"

"Girl?"

'The one who was killed last night."

"I'd heard of her."

"Will her death cause any complications for the studio?"

"What kind of complications?"

"You know, the shooting schedule, finding replacements."

"No, not really. She was a pretty minor player in the scheme of things. The complication for me is that it gives me more work to do. Which reminds me, as I was saying – "

"Yes, I know. You've got to run along." She shook her head back and forth slowly. "A sad, tragic thing, her death."

"Yes, I suppose so. But ours is a tough business, and sometimes trouble has a way of finding us whether we're ready for it or not."

"You put it very well."

Shellhammer got up from the table and gave her a peck on cheek. "But I do ramble on. Pay me no mention, my dear. The frustrated screenwriter in me bubbling up. I'll see you tonight."

He walked away and Liddy took a puff on her cigarette as she got back to the paper.

CHAPTER 9 : DEAD END

The neon light outside the dimly lit diner pulsated with a sad insistence in the early evening haze. Two nondescript figures sat in a booth by the window and attempted some conversation.

One of the men looked down at the newspaper and pointed. "I told you, Archer. Even the damn papers know. The story's been sent to the back pages."

"You said it."

"How's the coffee?"

"Terrible."

"I hear ya'. I've been to this place before. This cherry Coke is the only thing I can digest."

Fallon shuffled some papers spread over the table counter. "For the past couple days we've been doing all the right things. Talked to the executive producer and assistant, B unit director, head of security and his strongman, a few costars, the girl's parents. So the summary version: a B actress, Leena Sparkle, real name Margaret O'Halloran, winner of a lookalike contest and Kay Francis understudy, no enemies, no threats, no guy friends on the set, none that we know of anyway. We have to let this one go any minute." He looked down, frowned and rubbed his forehead. "Unless – "

"Unless what?"

"Just suppose, just suppose, mind you, that this Miss Sparkle wasn't the real target. Everybody said she was a lookalike for Kay Francis, won the contest and all that. What say?"

"What *are* you saying?"

"I'm saying I think it's time to pay another visit to the studio and talk to the queen of the lot herself."

CHAPTER 10 : THE POLICE
INTERROGATE THE QUEEN

Kay enjoyed a cigarette while she lounged on her dressing room sofa during mid-morning break. She was gobbling up her latest literary passion, the detective novel, this time Hammett's *The Maltese Falcon*.

A knock at her door.

"Police here to see you, Miss Francis."

"Police? What the devil do they want?"

"I don't know, ma'am. They just want to see you."

A long breath. "Oh, all right. Shoo them in."

In strode the two rather rumpled looking men. Both had baggy eyes and drooping faces, as though they'd already been awake all night. They seemed about forty and fit the part so well they could have been performing in a low budget crime movie.

The shorter man had a pug face which spoke of a rough background, perhaps as a boxer or soldier. He had an intense look in his eyes that suggested he used up huge reserves of energy to hold in his anger. The taller man had a calmer demeanor and a somewhat more polished appearance, if a beat detective can ever be polished. Both wore ordinary business suits topped off with well-worn fedoras and khaki overcoats. She noticed coffee stains on the shorter man's tie.

The taller man began to speak. "Miss Francis, I'm inspector Fallon and this is detective Sergeant Archer. Our many apologies for disturbing you here at work. We appreciate that you must be very busy."

"That's quite all right, inspector. How can I be of assistance?"

"I'll get to the point. We're investigating the Leena Sparkle murder that took place a few days ago here at the studio."

She shook her head back and forth. "Oh, yes. A tragic thing. A promising actress. But I don't understand. I wish to cooperate in any way possible, but what has it to do with me?"

The Sergeant reached into his overcoat pocket and pulled out a photo and handed it to her.

"You knew the woman?"

She examined the photo the handed it back to him casually.

"Yes. Well, sort of. I can't really say I knew her. I met her a few weeks ago. She won this Kay Francis look-alike contest. You know how the studios like to do these publicity things."

Inspector Fallon said, "Yes ma'am, we're aware of that part. The people over in personnel have been very helpful. We've been on the case for several days now and haven't gotten very far. Yes, it looks all the world like foul play; premeditation is written all over it."

Kay rubbed her eyes, then her forehead and turned

away. "But in what way can I help you? I didn't know the woman."

"That's sort of the whole point, ma'am. In our opinion the girl's death may have been a mistake." He glanced at his colleague and said, "What I mean is, we think you may have been the real target."

"What!?"

She walked over to the little bar and poured herself a small glass of whisky. "A little early," she said "but there you are." She raised the glass in the gesture of a toast. "Cheers."

"We've talked to the people in security. They tell us you've gotten threats. Letters."

"Yes. All the top stars get those. You know, crackpots, obsessed fans. It comes with the territory. I routinely turn them over to our security department and they take care of it."

"Yes, but some of these are death threats and they get pretty gruesome."

"Inspector, I understand your concern and believe me, I am touched, really. But I think your solicitude is misplaced."

"Strictly routine, miss. We have to follow all leads and we do have reason to believe there could be a little more here. This Leena Sparke, we can't find any motive for someone to kill her, and what we've found out tells us she not only looked like you, but copied everything about you: she already had your height and figure, she copied your hairstyle, your clothes, even your walk. And isn't that the exit you usually take, near where she was run over?"

"Well, yes. But not at that hour. You said she was killed around ten. I'm usually long home by that time getting ready for bed."

"A good point, but did the person driving the vehicle know that? But getting back to Miss Sparkle, what can you tell us about her?"

"I can't tell you much of anything. I only met her once. We posed for some pictures and shared a little small talk."

"Was there anything about her acquaintances or associates you remember? Boyfriends? Rivals? Anything like that."

"All I know is I heard something about her getting a job over on the B unit, part of the spoils for the competition victory. Some token bit parts. One has to start somewhere, you know. Anyway I'm sure they've got all the details over at the personnel and publicity departments."

"We've checked with them. Yes, we've verified the part about her acting career, such as it was. She was starting out but finally getting a few good supporting parts. It looks like she even wanted to copy your roles: society ladies, long suffering women, vamps, professional types."

"Very astute of you, inspector. Well, it's flattering she'd see me as a role model but again I think you're making too much of it."

"You may be right, but as I mentioned we have to look at all possible angles, however unlikely." He reached into his overcoat pocket and retrieved a business card and handed it to her. "Be sure to let us know if you think of anything else."

"I certainly will."

The men left and Kay glanced at her small desk. The morning mail had just arrived. One piece caught her eye. A telegram. She opened it and looked at the contents. Then she picked up the phone and dialed a familiar number.

CHAPTER 11 : THE RELUCTANT SLEUTH

As was his wont William Powell was dining alone between takes, sipping coffee and munching on a donut in the Warmer Bros. commissary. Befitting the uptown lawyer role he was currently playing, he was garbed in three-piece light grey herringbone suit and wore well-tended brogues. He affected a bemused concentration as he studiously perused the racing results from Santa Anita in the morning edition of *The Times*.

He paused to scan the large dining area. His gaze fixed on a small table over in a secluded corner near the stand where waitresses stacked dirty dishes. He recognized a second tier director who'd just had three failures in a row. Even with two months to go, his option was being dropped. He sat there alone, like a zombie, trying to nibble on his grilled cheese sandwich. Nobody came over to his table.

Then Powell noticed a lady over at the counter who'd been eyeing him carefully, and who now began walking in his direction. She proceeded slowly, cautiously. She was plain looking, a touch overweight, and dressed rather dowdy, so Powell divined she must have been from one of the technical departments. Certainly not a star. As she walked she glanced nervously aside as though looking for support from a companion in the wings.

She got to his table, smiled tensely and said, "Mr. Powell?"

Powell eyed her skeptically. "Yes?"

"I'm so happy to meet you, and I'm so nervous." She hesitated while she took in a few short breaths.

"Well?" said Powell.

"I'm Gloria Hufnagel, from the wardrobe department. I'm sure you've never met me or even heard of me."

Powell quizzically shook his head in the negative and his mouth opened slightly. *Another autograph seeker. Probably for her daughter. Oh well …*

"I have this personal matter," she said.

You see, I knew it.

Powell couldn't help noticing she was trying hard and meant well but her attempt at smiling as she spoke came out more as a grinning grimace.

She continued, "I haven't heard from my husband and I'm so worried."

Powell's eyes were beginning to glaze over but he managed a good natured, "Go on."

"Well, I' m hoping you can assist me in finding him."

Powell sat up in his chair. "Lady, just because I play detectives in the movies doesn't mean I do it in real life," he said, his voice more sharp edged.

"Oh, but they told me you were so understanding, and know all about these things."

"Who are *they*? And what are these things I'm supposed to know about?" He shook his head and held up his hand in a benevolent gesture. "Oh, never mind. Proceed."

"It is rather personal."

"It always is." A pause. "Really, Mrs. uh … "

"Hufnagel."

"Yes, of course. Mrs. Hufnagel, I think you've been misinformed. If you'll just talk to our security department."

"Oh no, Mr. Powell, that won't do at all. Just hear me out."

A long breath accompanied by a cross of the legs. "Okay, tell me your story."

"Well, you see, my husband disappeared about five days ago and – "

"Wait a minute," Powell snapped. "About five days ago? It's five days ago or not."

"That's the problem. I was visiting my sister up in Santa Barbara over the weekend, and when I got back he wasn't there, so I don't know exactly how long he's been gone."

"Okay, that sounds reasonable. And I do sympathize, Mrs. Heft … "

"Hufnagel."

"Yes, of course. Mrs. Hufnagel, really, I sympathize; I've had a wife or two walk out on me but they always come back."

Powell reached into his coat pocket and retrieved a business card. "Here's a guy I know. He's a good man, competent. He'll be able to help you out." He handed the card to her. It read ERNIE NOVEMBER, INVESTIGATIONS.

"Oh, no. I want you. You're the only one who can

help." She began to sob and took out a handkerchief and blew her nose.

Powell placed a comforting palm of his hand on her shoulder and said, "All right. Calm down. Tell me a little more."

And so she did. She summarized her husband's indiscretions, then branched out into their marital problems generally. Powell was about to nod off when he saw a young man with a serious look approach his table.

"Sorry to interrupt, sir. This message arrived for you. Says it's urgent." *My God, saved by the page boy.*

He looked at the lady and tried in his most sincere way, "I'm terribly sorry, ma'am. Your story is very interesting but I have to attend to this, and it can't wait. I'm sure your situation will work out."

"Thank you, Mr. Powell," she said.

Speaking into a nearby phone, Powell said rapid-fire, "I don't believe it. This is the second detective case I've been offered in the past fifteen minutes. Me, an actor. Anyway, what's it about? Oh, never mind. Why don't you just turn the whole thing over to the police? If these guys tried to kill you once – "

"But the warning. I don't like it, Bill. I don't like the smell of it. Something's not quite right."

"Okay. Meet me at the Brown Derby at noon and we'll talk about it. How's does that sound?"

"Bill, you're a peach. See you then."

Powell returned to the commissary to continue his coffee break cum breakfast. He had a look 'round and

Mrs. Hufnagel was nowhere to be found. With a sigh of relief he sat down, continued with his donut and coffee and got back to the *Times*.

Knowing Kay was a stickler for promptness, Powell appeared at the Brown Derby at eleven fifty-five. The *maître d'* led him to a choice table, where he demurred to the waiter's inquiry for anything to drink. He had a preliminary look around and liked what he saw: the Derby projected its confident, gleamingly polished air and he noticed the usual assortment of film types and various social climbers, all of whom wanted to see and be seen.

He especially admired the leather bar stools and the wall decorations which included signed pictures of stars, film industry executives and the obligatory good-old-days photos. Then his attention turned to the faux blonde at a nearby booth. She was wearing a pink satin dress and her platinum hair splashed against the mauve plush of the booth's back.

Outside, the cars that pulled up to the Derby were either oversize or new, usually both, and at exactly twelve o'clock the pale blue Cadillac appeared and stopped beside the entrance. Dressed in all whites, Kay got out while the driver whisked away the large vehicle to the parking area.

She entered and walked over to Powell's table. He arose, clasped both her hands and gave her a gentle kiss on the cheek. "Kay dear. Great to see you. Nice outfit."

"Thanks. I go to the tennis court right after this."

"Something to drink?"

"No, nothing."

Powell ordered himself a mineral water, then waved off the waiter. "By the way, if I may change the subject just a bit, I think we should pat ourselves on the back for the preliminary notices were getting for *One Way Passage*. They're especially fond of your performance."

"Thanks. That's awfully white of you to say so. I did so love the role. But they also said some nice things about you."

"Yes, I suppose they did. But getting back to the matter at hand: tell me what's going on."

She related the visit from the two detectives and what they'd told her. Then she said, "I don't know exactly what's happening. The police may be right in thinking I was the real target, but maybe our killer just wanted us to think that. Either way it makes me nervous. Who knows what this person wants or what he'll do next."

"Good point."

"Then there's this. It was delivered by Western Union this morning." She handed him an envelope. He took out the paper inside. Inside was a typewritten note on ordinary writing paper.

Get out of this picture if you know what's good for you.
   The Avenger

Powell affected a bemused grin "The guy's to the point, I'll give him that. Well, just turn it over to the police."

"I will. But I wanted you to see it."

"But is this avenger fellow for real? And is it

connected to the girl's murder? Or maybe – "

"Yes. Maybe just another crackpot."

Powell sipped his tonic water. "Well, what do you want me to do about it? Can't you manage your own snooping?"

"I'm busy with the picture and I don't want to be too obvious."

"Just hire a private detective. Who's that fellow you work with sometimes?"

"Johnny Caballero. Yes, he's very good. The only one I'd hire for something like this. But he's back in New York working on a case and won't be finished for at least two weeks."

"But I'm through with all this detective stuff. I just want to concentrate on other types of roles. And anyway I'm no sleuth in real life."

Her response was silence.

"Why me anyway?" he said as he took another sip of the tonic water.

"Because I trust you and you're discreet. And you have access to studio gossip, things the police won't find in personnel folders. Just a little legwork for me, please, please?"

"But Paramount's not even my studio anymore," Powell protested.

"Come on, Bill, you have lots of contacts there. And you know the ropes."

A sigh from Powell. "Okay. Where do I start?"

"With the source, of course."

Powell response was a blank stare. "The source?"

"The dead girl. Bill, you're a bit slow today."

"Sorry, my dear, too many martinis last night." A long breath from Powell. "Okay, I'll have a look see."

"With discretion," Kay said with index finger raised admonishingly.

Powell smiled and nodded. "With discretion."

A peck on Powell's cheek. "I knew you'd come through for me. You're a dear."

CHAPTER 12 : THE AGENT

His day at the studio now over, Powell could concentrate on the business of finding out about Leena Sparkle. She wasn't in the phone book or city directory under her professional name but a couple of well-placed phone calls did the trick. She lived in the Ravenswood Apartments over in the Hancock Park area. Powell raised an eyebrow and mused it was pretty tony digs for an understudy and B actress just starting out.

Another call yielded the girl's agent. Powell figured he had just enough time to whiz by and pay a visit. Twenty minutes later he parked his Packard near Ivar Street, about a half block from the agent's office on Cahuenga Boulevard.

The building was a medium size, well scrubbed structure in the grand classical style popular in the pre-Deco era. As he walked up to the entrance he noticed the huge door, over which was a fanlight and the name Lee Miller emboldened in black wooden letters severely stylized in arch Moderne. There were no other names on the outside, implying the agency took up the entire building.

Like many in the business Miller's was a professional moniker. His real name was Leskin Mickiewicz. He was from a family of Polish immigrants and had moved to Hollywood in the early Twenties. By now he was one of the more successful mid-range agents and Powell knew him mostly by what he'd heard: that Miller specialized in rising ingénues and, as agents went, had a reputation for honesty and being up front.

Powell opened the door and walked directly into the main reception room, which was a spacious, airy interior that occupied most of the first floor.

The furniture was Tudor revival in shades of brown and off-brown, and the color scheme extended to the thick brown curtains which adorned the wide windows. The perfectly scrubbed light grey tile floor was inlaid with small angels. Inside the waiting room sat lots of people, mostly young women, waiting to see Mr. Lee Miller. Some of those waiting were bubbly and alert. Some looked tired, as if they'd been there for days. And some looked just plain bored. Two lissome under secretaries sat at desks to the right. They perked up when they saw Powell enter.

The formidable secretary-in-chief loomed straight ahead. She was an intense-looking redhead with nails too long painted a shade too crimson. She was perched at a shining, light brown Deco style desk talking into an ivory white telephone. As soon as she saw Powell she said curtly into the phone, "Call you back."

She got up from her desk in a fluid movement. Her full height revealed a fleshy, statuesque frame as she beamed a wide smile and said, "Mr. Powell! It's so exciting, such an honor." Despite the animation her voice was little more than a sultry, loud whisper. She then walked around the desk to greet him with a discreet handshake and handclasp.

She was wearing a black wool skirt, pink silk blouse and black jacket with short sleeves, all rather tight fitting. Her outfit was punctuated by the flaming red shoes which packed what must have been three-inch heels. Her thick, wavy hair was perfectly coiffed in a longish style, and a showy collection of garish costume jewelry adorned her neck, wrists and fingers. With help of the high heels she towered over Powell, himself of man of rather impressive physical stature.

"I'm Lola Lolana, Mr. Miller's executive secretary," she said with a nervous smile and primp of her generous locks.

"I assure you the honor is mine, Miss Lolana." Powell clasped her hand and gave it a soft kiss. She responded with deep breath and barely audible sigh.

"To come to the point," Powell said, "I'd like to see Mr. Miller. Sorry I don't have an appointment but it is rather urgent."

"Oh, no appointment necessary. You'll have to see Mr. Hack first, just a formality, I assure you."

"Thanks." Powell hesitated, then said, "Don't you need to know what I want to see him about?"

"Not at all. I'm sure whatever your reason he'll want to see you. By the way I just saw *Jewel Robbery* last week. You were wonderful."

"Thanks. You're most kind."

Powell smiled good-naturedly and couldn't help wondering how long it would have taken to see Mr. Lee Miller if he hadn't been who he was. Oh well, the world was an unfair place, even in Hollywood.

Lola Lolana returned to her desk, picked up the phone and dialed a number, said Powell was there and 'yes' a couple of times. "He'll be right out," she exulted triumphantly.

Powell smiled and nodded but his attentions were on a tall, distinguished if none too happy-looking individual sitting stiffly over in the far corner. His white gloves, Bowler hat, silver-tipped cane and Savile Row attire suited him well. He let out a long breath, got up from his chair and strolled over to Miss Lolana's desk. He had a serious look on his face.

"I have been waiting three hours to see Mr. Miller." His voice was rich and sweet with cultivated British accent that oozed public school. "I'm not accustomed to waiting three hours to see anybody."

"So sorry, Mr. Filiba. Mr. Miller is just so busy today."

"And who is this gentleman, may I ask?" he said with a dismissive look in Powell's direction. "How is it he gets in right away?"

"Sir, please calm down."

"This is an outrage. The actor's union will hear about this, let me tell you." The man turned around and walked briskly out of the building.

"Tough day?" Powell said.

She flashed a toothy smile. "Oh, Mr. Powell, you're just too nice and understanding."

At that time a small, plump man, presumably Mr. Hack, appeared through a sliding side door and walked briskly in Powell's direction. The man wore a light grey three-piece silk suit a size too tight, which emphasized his rotund topography. He had a swarthy complexion with pock-marked face which was sweating noticeably. The bags under his eyes were dark, heavy and deep set. Powell noticed the man's off-blonde toupée which tilted at an awkward angle and didn't match his smoker's pallor, but the puffy style of the hair did give him an extra inch or so in height.

The man extended his hand and offered a handshake that was a little too insistent and with a grip too strong. "Mr. Powell. Indeed, an honor, sir. Sheldon Hack, Mr. Miller's executive assistant." He opened a gold cigarette case the size of a small briefcase. "Cigarette?"

"No, thanks. I have my own."

Hack withdrew a cigarette and began puffing away. As he spoke Hack coughed and gulped short breaths in between the smoking puffs. "Damn cigarettes will do me in yet. Sorry. To what do we owe the pleasure? No matter. My job is guardian of the gates but in your case you always have the keys. I'll take you straight away to Mr. Miller."

Hack led Powell to the elevator, which went up to the floor marked penthouse. They got out and walked down a long corridor. The walls were filled with glossy glamour photos of women, presumably Miller's clients. They all looked more or less alike except for the color of the hair and tilt of the head. Powell didn't see anyone

51

who resembled Leena Sparkle and wondered why her picture wasn't out there with the other starlets.

Powell followed Hack along the corridor through double doors into an outer office with three secretaries, then past them towards more double doors of heavy black glass with martial-looking gold eagles etched into the panels.

They went down three steps covered with carpet. The feet sank into the cushy material, at least two inches worth. Hack pressed a button in the paneling and a door slid open noiselessly, revealing what must have been Miller's office. The high ceilinged space was the size of a small tennis court and floated out to a balcony which offered a wide view of Los Angeles and environs. A fully stocked bar rested on one side of the room, next to it a small fireplace. A white grand piano glistened in the far corner. Like the reception area the floor was tile. The furniture was severe, ultra modern bleached white, the desk just a little smaller than a Brinks truck.

Miller was sitting in a tall chair at the far edge of the room with a white sheet over him while a barber clipped his hair. Meanwhile two young women tended to his fingernails and toenails. A thick cigar dangled from the side of his mouth and a tiny thread of smoke wisped from the end of the cigar and wafted upwards.

As soon as he saw Powell Miller bounded up and tossed off the sheet. Underneath he was wearing a tee shirt and dress slacks. He then waved off the help with a sweep of his arm in the manner of a Persian pasha dismissing slaves. His generous hand revealed long, tentacle-like fingers weighted down by diamond rings that gleamed like searchlights. The barber and two girls left quietly. Hack lingered for a few seconds, then per a nod from Miller, left reluctantly.

"William Powell! Pardon my appearance. You caught me at … well, they told me you were here. An honor, sir." As he spoke he put on thick, dark rimmed glasses and busily attired himself in a tan Arrow dress shirt. Then he faced Powell and extended his hand. Like Hack's, Miller's handshake was vigorous and his grip tight. Miller was tall, wiry, athletic in an elegant sort of way, with flawless posture. He had fine, perfectly trimmed chestnut brown hair that might have glowed in the dark. His skin was soft and fresh; it looked like warm milk on a summer evening. He was of indeterminate age, maybe forty or fifty. Unlike Hack, his hazel eyes were alert and penetrating, but they gave away no expression, not cold really, just neutral.

"It's quite flattering," Powell said. "Everyone at your office thinks it's an honor to meet me."

"Because it is." Miller puffed on his cigar and his voice lowered to a near whisper as he said conspiratorially, "Truth be told, we don't get many stars of your caliber here. Drink?"

"No, thanks. I can only stay a minute"

Miller walked over to the bar, poured himself a glass of brandy, lifted the glass, sniffed and took an initial sip. "I have it flown in from Paris. And they get it direct from the Crimea."

"Most impressive."

"How can I help you? Anything, just say it."

"I've, shall we say, taken an interest in one of your protégés, Leena Sparkle, the girl who was killed over at Paramount." Powell spoke his words slowly, carefully.

"And this. I'd appreciate it if my inquiries are kept on the q.t."

Miller's face went blank for a moment, but he quickly returned to form. "Sure. If anyone asks, which they won't, I'll just say you were doing a favor for a friend, looking for an agent."

"Thanks. Much obliged."

"Don't mention it." Miller looked down and shook his head back and forth pensively. "Terrible, tragic thing. When I heard about it I broke down and wept, I kid you not. I know what you're thinking. Under that tough exterior beats a heart of stone. Crocodile tears. Well, I was genuinely fond of the girl."

Miller took a long puff on his cigar and exhaled. The smoke danced in the air for a moment, then disappeared through the slits of the ventilation machine. He then continued his monologue, praising Leena Sparkle's star power and acting potential.

As Miller spoke Powell looked at the innumerable photos of stars and movie industry players on the walls, all addressed to Lee Miller with love and kisses or something to that effect. One of the pictures caught his eye. It was of Miller with a young woman at a dinner party or night club. The woman bore an uncanny resemblance to Kay Francis. Powell figured she had to be Leena Sparkle. The photograph was inscribed. Powell just made out the wavy handwriting: *To Lee, Love forever, Leena.*

"Thanks for the comments. Fascinating," Powell said. "But here's what I'm interested in. What did you know about the girl personally? Who would be sore enough at her to do something like this?"

Miller frowned and looked away. "I didn't really know her. I don't get involved in my clients' personal lives. Okay, I admit it. Sometimes I go out with my actresses, the real promising ones, mostly to see and be seen, photographs, that sort of thing. It's all part of the game. But nothing untoward, I assure you. I'm a family man, wife and kids."

"Nothing untoward inferred. By the way, did you ever go out with Leena Sparkle?"

"Yeah, maybe once. But again, just for show. Nothing going on."

"Of course not. By the way I didn't see her picture out there with the others on the walls."

"Yeah, she was there before but I took her picture down. I didn't think it was good form to keep her photo on the wall. But I kept the one in here, a little sentiment and all that."

"Perfectly understandable."

"Anyway, I can get you her address and phone number."

"Thanks, but I have those already."

"Tell you the God's honest truth I think they were wasting her talent in those bit parts and low grade B films." Miller looked back and forth stealthily as though making sure no one was listening. "Don't tell anyone I said so, but the story was Lubitsch was grooming her for the big time, she was a kind of ... well, he took what you might call a special interest in her. She was a real comer, you know, had that something extra. Very sad."

"Naturally you would want to think so, being who you are. If she hit it big it would feather your cap something proud."

Miller opened his hands in an imploring gesture. "What can I say? I'm a hundred percent agent."

"What about boyfriends, that sort of thing?"

Again the imploring hands. "I got so many starlets I couldn't keep their social lives straight even if I tried. As for the girl, can't help you there."

"Well, thanks for the information anyway."

"Sure thing." Miller got out a gold trimmed, monogrammed business card of high quality stock and gave it to Powell. "My direct number here, and my home phone number too. Anytime, day or night, at your service."

"Thanks. Most appreciated."

"Find your way out okay? I can call Sheldon or one of the girls."

"Not necessary. I think I can manage. Thanks for your time and assistance."

Powell walked past the same three secretaries outside Miller's office. They eyed him with curiosity. When he got to the bottom floor he managed to avoid a second encounter with Sheldon Hack as he strolled through the reception area in best unobtrusive manner.

There were still lots of people sitting around waiting. As he got to the exit he looked back. The two under secretaries gave him their fifty-cent smiles but Miss Lola Lolana was the sun herself. She stood up and beamed. Her whole body seemed to glow and her wide smile showed off her perfect, whiter-than-white teeth. The smile seemed genuine, and she offered a sprightly wave to him. Powell appreciated the attention. He smiled, nodded and tipped his hat to her as he exited the building.

CHAPTER 13 : CASING THE APARTMENT

Shiny and stylish, the eight story modernist structure cut an impressive figure in the evening twilight. Its off-white Deco bonafides leapt out almost too proudly while a collection of symmetrically placed palm trees and cypress pines adorned the grounds just outside the building.

As he entered the lobby Powell admired the terrazzo floors and vaulted ceilings but caught a whiff of dank cigar smoke which hung over the well-tended furnishings. The plump, beautifully attired woman at the front desk smiled broadly as he approached her. As he got closer he noticed the lady's rouge-smeared cheeks and even more so her cheap perfume which suddenly drenched him in a choking, pungent cloud.

"Hello," he said, suppressing a cough and wheezy breathing.

She hesitated as she began to speak, "Forgive me for asking, aren't you … "

"Yes, I am. And I'm very flattered you recognize

me. You'd be surprised how often I go out in public and people don't bat an eye."

"Oh, it's so exciting. We get a few film types here but no one of your caliber, Mr. Colman. By the way my name's Polly."

At least they knew who I was at the agent's office. Okay, Powell, just calm down. Ronald Colman for a night if that's what it takes. Powell tipped his hat and nodded. "Pleased to meet you, Polly. An honor indeed."

She frowned and shook her head. "But that sad business about the young actress who lived here."

"Yes, I heard about that." He puckered his lips in sympathetic mode and looked down, shaking his head back and forth. "A promising career cut tragically short. But, more happily," he said as his voice perked up, "I'm here on a little personal matter. My contact doesn't want his, or her, name revealed. A woman of your caliber will understand, I'm sure. If you could just buzz me through."

"Oh, it's against the rules." She looked around and smiled, eyebrows raised, "but considering it's you, we'll just bend the rules this one time."

"You're a dear," Powell said.

The lady pressed the release to the gated part of the building and Powell entered gingerly.

After a little fiddling with his special key Powell felt the door latch release. He carefully turned the knob, gave a nudge to the door and crept in. The drapes were open. Through the oversize windows the lights of Los Angeles beckoned like the Milky Way on a clear night.

He took out his small flashlight and began to have a look 'round. The spacious apartment was neatly organized, everything in its place. Either Leena Sparke was a tidy housekeeper or a maid came in a few days a week. It looked as though nothing had been disturbed. If the cops had already been there they cased the place using kid gloves.

The apartment was tastefully decorated in a Spanish Deco style which favored tile instead of carpet. Pictures of what were likely the parents were perched on a desk in the far corner of the living room.

He then went into the bedroom. The first thing he noticed was a signed framed photo of George Brent on the night table. Powell grunted as he picked up the photo and eyed it warily. *First Colman now Brent. Well, he's a handsome enough fellow, and a good actor.* He put the picture back and continued his inspection. A collection of neatly arranged books lined the shelves of the bedroom far wall. He noted the smattering of philosophy and history titles interspersed within the expected books on acting and modern fiction.

The large walk-in closet got his attention, in particular the plethora of high quality clothes: dresses, gowns, skirts, tennis and riding outfits. Many of the clothes had a Paris chic quality about them.

He flipped through the pages on the desk calendar and found handwriting on the date following her murder. It was scrawled, 'B.E. 10:00'.

Then a sound of the door opening. The lights went on. "OK! Hold it right there!"

CHAPTER 14 : EVEN SAM SPADE SOMETIMES WENT TO JAIL

The smell of stale tobacco and human sweat clung to the walls and furniture of the little room which barely had enough space for a small table, two chairs and a tiny filing cabinet.

Detective Sergeant Archer's voice spoke of fatigue and frustration as he addressed his well-manicured prisoner. "C'mon Powell, give. We don't want to go through this again. What were you doin' in that girl's place?" He pronounced the words in the last sentence with a slow insistence.

"You tell me," Powell said in breezy but focused delivery.

"Here's what I'll tell ya: you and the girl had a thing goin' and you were there to steal away any incriminating stuff, love letters and such."

"Sounds exciting," Powell said as he sat calmly, his demeanor a combination of entertained and bored.

"Try this for exciting. Looks like the girl just got to

be too much of a luxury and you had to take measures."

"Measures? You guys read too many pulp magazines. That's why you talk so tough. Speaking of reading material, could you fetch me a copy of *Harper's?* I need some mental stimulation. Your routine wears a little thin."

"Don't crack wise with us fella. You may be a hot shot movie star and all that, but this time we got you dead to rights and you know it."

"Better check that thought, Archer," Fallon said as he entered the room. He nodded toward the outside then said, "Powell, you got company. Looks like the cavalry just arrived."

As the two men were leaving the room Powell said with his trademark suave grin, "Be seein' ya, boys."

Kay Francis entered the little room. "Bill, I just couldn't believe it when I heard. How did you get into this fix?"

"Just lucky, I guess. By the way, how in blazes did you manage your way back here?"

"I told them I was acting in your capacity as attorney. The red cheeked fellow at the front desk was so star struck he didn't check my story."

"You're a clever girl."

"Thanks. By the way, did you tell them you're, as it were, working for me?"

"Of course not. They think I killed the girl."

Kay let out a nervous chuckle. "Anyway, help is on the way. I made a call to Paramount's Mr. Fix-it. One of his legal eagles should be here any second."

Sure enough Nelson Charalambides appeared a few minutes later and met them in the small interrogation room. He wore a light brown vicuna suit which looked good on his wiry frame, and his tanned, handsome face suggested he spent plenty of time on the golf course and tennis court. He was one of the top luminaries in the studio's formidable legal department, and his good looks and athleticism probably served him well in the courtroom.

He vigorously shook hands with them as he said, "Hello, Mr. Powell, Miss Francis. Good to see you. Mr. Shellhammer assured me this is just one big misunderstanding. I'm sure we can sort it all out. I'll be talking with the Commissioner any minute. We'll have you out of here in no time."

Powell and Kay had reason to be confident in his assessment. Charalambides and his colleagues all had a magician-like skill at making problems go away when stars or executives ran afoul of the law.

If things got dicier the studio could call on the heavy legal artillery, guys like Gerald Fiedler or Harrison Tumworth. But most of the time the legal boys, under Shellhammer's watchful eye, could make short work of compromising situations. Nobody wanted to know the how; the only concern was results.

"You just hang on and we'll straighten things out. The press hasn't got wind of this yet and we'll do our best to maintain that status. You'll hear from me soon." As he closed the door he flashed a tense smile that seemed to take lots of effort to produce.

"Kind of has a way with the patter," Powell said.

"Downright gives you a warm feeling all over."

"I don't like him. But they say he gets results."

"Yeah. So does Al Capone. Anyhow, I presume I'll be out of here in an hour or so. And thanks for coming down."

"Don't mention it."

"I've got a lead."

"What's that?"

"Meet me at BE's tomorrow night at ten and we'll see."

"Sure. What's BE's?"

"Big Eddie's. It's over in an alley off Cosmo Street, near BBB's Cellar."

"I know where it is. Why didn't you say so straight away?"

"My little joke. It was the girl's shorthand." He handed her the piece of paper he'd torn from the desk calendar. "It was right there on her living room desk, staring at me like a ripe piece of cheese in a mousetrap, just waiting for me. So I helped myself. Yes, I got caught in the process but our legal boy will fix things. Anyhow she was supposed to go to Eddie's the very next day but was inconvenienced by a speeding car. I've got a feeling it's worth a visit. I know a guy there."

"Naught, naughty. Pilfering evidence," she said as she waved an accusatory finger.

"Yeah. Well, the police won't notice and anyway remember the old saying what they don't know can't hurt them."

CHAPTER 15 : SPEAKING EASY
AT BIG EDDIE'S

The scrim of cigarette smoke hung overhead like billowy clouds on a summer evening. The smell of women's perfume oozed through the moist air, mixing in with the faint aroma of spilt gin. Big Eddie's was crowded, and why not. It had all the accouterments of a self-respecting, well-appointed speakeasy: long bar, tables, full show orchestra, samba music purring unobtrusively while stylish couples caressed the dance floor. The clientele included a lavender mixture of ambiguous types who spiced the proceedings.

The *maître d'* recognized Powell and Kay as they approached the entrance. "Right this way for the VIPs," he said in a blustery voice.

He took them to a choice table near the dance floor. A few peering eyes noticed but mostly the folks paid no attention, preoccupied as they were with themselves and their own affairs. And besides, they'd seen film stars before.

"Where's Eddie?" Powell said.

"He's down in Tijuana looking at horses. You know how he loves the races."

"Yes, I sort of like them myself."

"Here's your spot. The best in the house." He made welcoming flourish with his arm.

"Thanks, most hospitable to a first-time guest," Powell said as he slipped the man a five dollar bill.

After they'd settled in Kay said, "Interesting club. I've heard of it but my first time here. By the way, what do you think we'll find?" she said as she took out a cigarette and lit it.

"I don't know. That's why I'm here. The BE's on her calendar had to be this place. The straight dope is this is where the film people and the hard guys like to mix. Somehow it fits in with the girl's fashionable digs and her not-so-fashionable exit."

"Sounds reasonable."

"There's Joey Chicago," Powell said as he waved and nodded.

Joey made a curt goodbye to his company at the bar and headed over in their direction, moving in a walk that was more of a slither. He was decked out in snappy fedora and brown suit, the most notable feature being the long jacket with wide lapels and broad, padded shoulders.

"Hi, Joey. How's business?"

Joey reached their table and greeted them with a wide smile which revealed a full set of unruly teeth. He began with some giggle-coated laughter, then said, "Well, if ain't Tommy and Tuppence. When you told me what you was doin' I thought, you people gotta stop mixin' fact and fiction."

"Okay, Joey, you got in your bon mot," Powell said.

"Ban what?"

"Never mind. Now what about the girl?" Powell took out a glossy and handed it to Joey, who looked at the picture and affected a studious frown that seemed strangely incongruous on his rough-edged face which sported a scar across his left eyebrow.

Joey examined the photo as a waiter brought over some drinks and presented them to Powell and Kay with a triumphant, "Management says it's on the house."

Kay took a swig, made a grimace and shivered as she shook her head back and forth in a rapid motion

"It has a kick to it, eh?" Powell said.

"Ugggh … tastes like gasoline warmed over."

"But it'll make the world look better." Powell turned toward Joey and said, "Well, Joey, do you recognize her?"

"Sure, she liked to come in here, but I don't know nothin' about a Leena Sparkle. This woman called herself … Janet. Yeah, that's it. Janet Henry. She liked her cigarettes and liquor, but insisted on the high-class stuff. Danced a little bit."

Powell hesitated, mouth slightly open. Then he said, "Is that supposed to be a joke?"

"What kind of a joke?

"The name."

"It's a perfectly good name, suited her swell. Anyhow she liked to come in and chum around. Real sociable. She was usually with some mucky muck lookin' types, sharp dressers. She acted pretty cozy with them. They looked like tough guys to me but they could've been movie executives, not the top but middle men, you know, the flunkies and yes men."

"Interesting," Powell said as he stirred his cocktail. "Why do they keep putting these oversize olives into my drink? Didn't I ask for a lemon twist? Oh, well, what can you expect from a speakeasy, even a high class one. Sorry. Go on."

Joey seemed distracted by Powell's critique but continued, "There was a ruckus one night when a pretty boy – you know the type – comes in with a twist on his arm. Classy lookin' dame. Turns out the dame took an instant dislike to Janet, or whatever you said her name was. Anyhow she acted like she knew her, and wasn't none too happy about it. There was a lotta shoutin'. I was over by the bar. I didn't hear nothin', you know, just sort of observed. But I did catch when she screams 'You stay away from my husband, you hear, or something bad will happen to you'."

"You didn't recognize the woman who made the threats?"

"No, sorry. She come in before but I don't know who she was. She always had these poofy characters with her, you know, hangin' on her arm, sometimes two or three at a time. They treated her real nice, genteel. She danced a lot, really liked it. The guys with her were good dancers, too. She always behaved herself real good except that one time."

Joey took out a cigarette and lit it, breathed in a deep puff, then said, "Oh, and one other thing. One time I overheard this Janet dame havin' what you'd call a disagreement with a guy. Real heated. I didn't catch everything but got the drift."

He took another drag on his cigarette and had a swig of cognac. "She doused him with the whisky in her glass, then said somethin' like, 'Why are you making such a fuss? What's a few dollars among friends? And don't try to get tough with me. Remember, I know things'. Then the bouncers came and broke 'em up. She had quite a bit to drink and she said things like that before, so I paid it no mind, but this time it was more intense. I thought you might find it interesting."

"Who was the man?" Powell said.

"Don't know. Never saw him before. Tall, sorta wholesome lookin'. Nice dresser, but not as flashy as lots of guys who come in here."

"What did the man say to her?"

"Something like 'take it easy'."

Powell took a sip on his drink and reached into his pocket. "Thanks much, Joey. This is all great stuff."

Powell placed a hundred dollar bill in Joey's palm as they shook hands.

"Just a minute, Joey," Kay said. "Here's a little something else." She took out five crisp one hundred dollar bills and placed them in his hand. "Do what you have to, turn L.A. upside down, but find out who that man was."

For once Joey was speechless. He sufficed with a thin smile and a "Thanks." Then he closed his palm, placed the money in his coat pocket and departed straight away.

Powell looked at Kay and said, "What say we get out of here. Somewhere we can think and talk. Derby?"

"The Derby it is."

They sat in a secluded corner and nursed their tonic waters.

"Your friend Joey is quite the character."

"Yes. A bit volatile but a good source for information you can't find elsewhere. You think there's really something there, enough to pay him five C-notes? Isn't it possible the girl was just trying to welch on money she owed the guy?"

"It's not the money part that bothers me. It's the other thing she said, about her knowing things."

"She was lubricated. Probably all bluff."

"Could be. But I'll be very interested in what Joey finds out."

"Well, it's your money. Otherwise, we know this Leena girl, or Janet Henry, or whoever she was, visited the club and didn't make any secret she liked to associate with shady types. Her death may have something to do with said associations, and may not."

Kay jumped in: "Also, we found out about a woman, identity unknown, who threatened her."

"Exactly. But why not the same interest in the woman as in the mystery man? They both had their issues with the girl."

"Good question. Something tells me the answer's not so simple as a jealous wife doing in the girl. No, it's got to have a connection with the studio."

"A logical conclusion. But in other ways we're none the wiser."

'None the wiser perhaps, but – "

"Yes?"

"Bill, I've got an idea. I'll throw a shindig, a big to-do at my house, to brighten spirits. I've a rep for good parties. People will come. Something may shake loose, a little too much alcohol, slip of the tongue, that sort of thing. You'll be my eyes and ears. This Sunday. The folks are used to short notice."

CHAPTER 16 : GARDEN PARTY

Lots and lots of beautiful people. Vintage early autumn Southern California weather: warm, clear skied, the faintest hint of a coolish breeze. The champagne flowed and caviar piled up in abundance. The lavish flower arrangements, well-manicured grounds and cocktail piano music which floated in the background added the necessary aesthetic exclamation points.

Resplendent in white Vionnet afternoon dress, her sleek new secretary in tow, Kay mingled triumphantly. She loved to lord over these affairs. The beau monde guests tried to suppress their stares and sufficed with the occasional murmur. She overheard the random 'she calls him her secretary,' but undaunted she glided on, gently dragging her protégé by the slightest edge of his thumb. It didn't matter a whit to her that some must have been wondering why this escort and not her husband.

As she walked with her employee close by, she further scanned the crowd. Her eyes fixed at the caviar table as she caught the visage of Mercedes de Acosta, she of the close-cropped jet black hair which so resembled her own. *How did I miss her when she arrived?* With the skill of a true coquette, Mercedes was fending off a small group of male admirers who hung on her every pronouncement. Kay noted with pleasure that one of the admirers was Mercedes's old friend Igor Stravinsky, himself a much sought after attendee for such affairs.

As she weaved through the crowd Kay noticed an obligatory invitee, a powerful critic she always did her best to ingratiate. The woman was wearing a short chinchilla coat that must have been impossibly hot in the full afternoon sun. The woman's husband, a noted surgeon, was passed out on a lounge chair, likely overcome by alcohol. His fondness for drink was well known, and Kay overheard the woman say to a nearby companion, "Oh, don't disturb him. He needs the rest. He has two operations tomorrow morning."

Most of Paramount's top brass was there too, and she'd paid due tribute to them. In fact, some had already left. So no surprise when she saw Gordon Shellhammer at the patio entrance, fetching escort on his arm. Kay noticed right away the woman wasn't his wife. She excused herself from René and the small group clustered around her, then strolled over in Shellhammer's direction. He wasn't quite top-level studio royalty but she felt a certain obligation given his nick-of-time pulling of strings the other night.

His official title was special assistant to the executive producer but his real job was being management's eyes and ears. He lurked around the various sets looking for fires to put out and also arranged the occasional party and publicity event, and he frequently offered a sympathetic ear to the complaints of directors and stars. But his real specialty was the sticky legal and police issues, and he usually delivered, even if it was the lawyers who did the dirty work.

She managed a warm smile as she said, "Gordon, so glad you could make it."

He smiled, clasped her hand gently and gave it a discreet kiss. Shellhammer wore his fortyish years lightly. His near film star looks included a smoothly chiseled face and a thick mop of dark hair which he combed straight back. His blue sport jacket and white slacks looked good on his six feet one inch frame. "A true honor, Kay. You grace me as always with your generous invitation. Such a beautiful house. And your grounds. All very opulent."

"You're just too kind, Gordon."

Shellhammer quickly made a gesture toward the stunning woman at his side. "Let me introduce my new administrative assistant, Miss Carmen Dravago."

He presented the woman in the manner of a father showing off a daughter. But this woman wasn't his daughter. Carmen Dravago was a dark beauty, maybe thirty years old, medium height with sharply defined features, looking smashing in pink Chanel day suit which accentuated her smoky skin tones.

"Honored, I'm sure, Miss Francis," she answered in a voice both well modulated and edgy.

Kay hesitated. It was the girl's eyes. The nervous intensity belied the affable manner. But her looks were just the ticket. Like all the front office types Gordon liked the ladies and Kay pondered the inevitable question: was she or wasn't she? But then again, she mused, who was she to ponder? Amidst all her thoughts she managed a diplomatic, "Not at all. It is I who am honored. And, please, call me Kay. Gordon, my compliments on your choice of new assistant."

"Thanks, Kay. Your blessing is always important to me. Once again, wonderful affair. Yours are the gold standard of garden parties. Looks like everybody from the studio is here. Thanks for inviting me. It gets our mind off, well … "

"I know, Gordon. Thanks for coming."

He excused himself gracefully and he and his escort began to mingle. Finally she was free to further scan the crowd. She saw Sam Raphaelson, the film's screenwriter, talking with a small cadre of literary types. She may have caught the visage of Dashiell Hammett amongst the literati – she had invited him, after all – but she wasn't sure it was him. Most of all she also noticed the conspicuous absence of Miriam Hopkins and Ernst Lubitsch.

She glanced across the lawn and saw Herbert Marshall, accompanied by his wife, who kept a close watch on him but also seemed to be looking in her direction constantly. *Hmm … does she know?* Kay noticed Marshall surreptitiously eyeing the well-built redhead in tight fitting dress nearby and mused with some satisfaction that with the wife on his arm all he could do was look.

Her thoughts were interrupted by anther guest who just arrived, Dixon Peele, head of security, glum and intense as always. She greeted him blandly and he took his leave. He was followed by Frank Lugg, his top Lieutenant and made-to-order tough guy. But this time he was looking elegant in red blazer, and his persona was softer than usual. She got the explanation fast.

"This is my daughter," he said, his wide smile speaking lots of pride. "Thanks for allowing me to bring her. She's so excited."

She clasped the girl's hand and gave her a soft peck on the cheek. "Enchanté. You're so pretty. You have a career as an actress, I'm sure."

"Oh, Miss Francis, you're too kind," she said in a polished, measured voice. "But I'm studying law at university actually."

"Law?" Kay responded. Her mouth puckered as she said the word, but she recovered quickly and managed a warm smile as she said, "Well, don't you think it's time to start laying down the law? Please mingle and enjoy the food and champagne."

"Thanks," she said.

Signaling he was pleased with the encounter, Lugg looked back to her, smiled and nodded as he walked away.

Then she noticed her ever capable lawyer Gerald Fielder walking in her direction, per usual sporting his trademark enigmatic smile. He looked the part with his round, reddish face, balding hairline, and portly physique which filled out his dark grey pinstriped suit.

"Wonderful party, Kay. But may I have a word with you?"

"Yes?"

"Privately."

"Not now, Gerald. Can't you see I must attend to my guests?"

"It is rather important. I'm afraid I must insist."

A long sigh, then, "Oh, all right. I must take my leave."

She made a few perfunctory excuses to the guests nearby, then took Mr. Leclair's hand and led him over to Fielder.

"Harry, may I present Mr. Leclair, my new secretary. Mr. Leclair, this is Gerald Fiedler, my attorney."

Leclair extended his hand, which Fielder refused to shake.

Fielder sufficed with a curt, "Tell me, Kay, are you in the habit of inviting the hired help to your parties?"

Her eyes widened and her smile vanished. "You'll excuse us, Mr. Leclair, as we seem to have run out of small talk."

She and Fiedler walked back to the house and entered the living room, which was vacant.

"Really, Gerry, that was totally unforgiveable. Just because you're a well-connected lawyer doesn't allow you to forget basic courtesies."

He took a breath, about to reply, but she continued, "As for Mr. Leclair being hired help, I place him on the same level as that of my agent, business manager, and for that matter, legal and financial advisors, all of whom received invitations to this party. Does that answer your question about inviting hired help?"

Fiedler looked stunned. Rarely for him, he had no verbal comeback.

"Now what is it that's so important?"

Fielder quickly returned to form. "Kay, I've been your personal and professional legal advisor for ... how long has it been now?"

"A little over four years," she said as she took a deep breath and looked away. *Seems I've heard this conversation before.*

"And your interests are always supremely imperative for me, and let me add, in not too self congratulatory fashion, I can say that I've served those interests well. And let me further point out that I have the greatest respect for your privacy, and that I would not interrupt you at such an important occasion – "

"Not to be abrupt, Gerald, but, again, I have guests. So could you get to the point?"

"Very well. My dear Kay, you have been exceptionally astute with your finances. A far be it for me to question you."

I hear a however coming …

"However – "

See. I told you.

Fiedler continued, "Recent developments in that area have given me pause and compel me to offer a few words of guidance."

Kay took in and let out another long breath. "Gerald, I'm touched by your solicitude, but once again, could you get on with it?"

"Yes, I understand. The point is your Mr. Lecalir. Who is he? How long have you known him? What do you know about his background? What does he want?" Fielder's words flowed in quintessentially legalistic, heavy-handed style.

"He's a screenwriter. I met him at a party, if you must know."

"Screenwriter," he harrumphed, not bothering to hide the sarcasm in his voice. "What has he written? Where did he study?"

"What does all that matter? He's having a slow spell in his work, so I hired him on as secretary. And I might add he's doing a great job, just a whiz with the numbers and paperwork."

"The numbers are what I'm concerned about."

"Could you be more specific?"

"Indeed. To be more specific: during a routine examination of your financial affairs in my capacity as power of attorney, I've noticed you've given this Mister Leclair much discretion in your financial matters, and he's made some questionable redistribution of assets and investments. Need I remind you that even though you're a wealthy woman by dint of your status as a film star, in these times one must be prudent."

"Thank you for the concern but – "

Fiedler rather unchivalrously interrupted, "Moreover, he's made several large withdrawals in recent days from your checking account, to which you seem to have given him unfettered access. A thousand dollars last week, three thousand two days ago, and two thousand just – "

"I'm well aware of Mr. Leclair's withdrawals. He has a salary to cover, incidental expenses as well. And besides, he pays some bills for me. Some people prefer cash. All these withdrawals are in his capacity as secretary, thus I consider these transactions, of which you so obviously disapprove, in the way of doing his job and assisting me. If you have any questions I'll call him right away and you may express your concerns directly."

"That won't be necessary. I've just wanted to point out certain facts."

"Gerald, you are a dear, and a fine lawyer, and I'm sure you mean well. Your concerns are appreciated and believe me, I'm grateful for your loyalty, but I don't think we need to pursue this line of conversation any further."

"As you wish," he said with a bow as he left the room and walked toward the hors d'oeuvres table.

Kay walked slowly back toward the outside and her guests. William Powell greeted her at the patio door.

"What do you think so far?" she said. "Anything suspicious?"

"With this crowd, everybody and nobody is suspicious."

"And all those security men hovering about. I don't like it; they don't fit in. But the studio insisted. Keep a watch on them."

"Will do."

She looked to her side and, much to her delight, there was Percy Doveless, theatre critic and book reviewer extraordinaire. He was decked out in customary cream-colored suit with red tie and white Panama hat.

"Percy! So glad you made it."

"Of course, my sweet. How could I miss this party?" Percy bowed as he took her hand and gave it a gallant kiss. "You look just smashing, as always."

"Thanks."

"And your guests are simply marvelous." He exaggerated the word as 'mahvelous'. "Is that Scott and Zelda Fitzgerald over there? I'd love to meet them but I must tread lightly; I was a wee bit rough on his last book. Oh, but first, I just have to talk to Mae Clark. She's so gorgeous. And looking so stunning today." He placed both palms of his hands over his chest and let out a breath. "I'm almost too shy."

"Percy, you devil, you're getting downright broad-minded."

"Well, dearie, if the shoe fits," he said as he sauntered away.

Then, unexpected, there emerged from the living room door, to a wave of whispers and stares, the final elegant touch, the great Noel Coward himself, impeccable as always. He wore a light grey blazer, white slacks and silk tie, all of which looked like he'd purchased fifteen minutes ago. In one hand he held the ever present cigarette and in the other a cocktail.

Kay saw him and immediately strode over in his direction. She greeted him with an air-kiss and handclasp. "Noel, I'm so glad you're here. Truly you're the prestige guest among prestige guests."

"Nonsense, my dear Kay. There are more stars present than in the heavens. I'm just a minor constellation. Tell you the truth, I'm not much for these Hollywood affairs. I'd rather be home having scones and warm milk with my dear grandma-ma. By the way, is it true Greta Garbo will be attending?"

He whispered something in her ear. She giggled, affected a mock startled pose and flicked her fan in his direction. "Oh, Noel, you're just too naughty."

Then she shrugged. "Anyway, as for her presence here, your guess is as good as mine. I sent her an invitation but got no response, and you know how she likes to cancel. She's not much of a party animal."

"Well, Garbo or no Garbo, splendid party, Kay darling. As always you outdo yourself with the extravagance. You know," he said, waving an accusatory finger, "when the proletariat takes over, and they will, just you see, they'll line us up against the wall and shoot us all." He raised his cocktail glass. "Chin-chin."

"Speak for yourself, Noel. I've already been chastised for allowing hired help to attend the party, so my sympathies are clearly with the people."

Powell was standing nearby and jumped in. "I think Noel's idea is swell." He raised his glass and said, "I'll second it."

Kay said, "Well, if you can't beat 'em – " She held up her champagne glass and declared, "The revolution!"

The guests joined in with a tinkling of glasses. "The revolution! The revolution," along with a few choruses of "Hear, hear."

All the guests had left and Powell and Kay sat on the living room sofa.

She mused philosophical. "The party was an artistic success."

"That means we don't know a lot more than we did before the party. At least you've not gotten any more threatening notes from that Avenger fellow."

"That's something to be grateful for, I suppose. What do you make of Gordon's new assistant?"

"Hard to tell. I couldn't get a word in edgewise with all the admirers clustered around her. But I talked to him a bit. He apologized profusely about the wife not attending, something about keeping her date at the Coconut Grove with girlfriends and the male cuties who escort her to such places. He didn't seem to take any exception."

"Not overly enlightening, I'm afraid."

"But I may have some consolation for you: I've done a little more snooping, on my own."

"Bill, you've been holding out on me. Shame on you."

"Yes, my dear, but I wanted to keep it under wraps until the party, to see if anything played out."

"Well, what have you got?"

"Among other things, there's that agent of hers. Playing his cards pretty close to the vest, he is. I'm sure he knows stuff he's not telling me."

"That's an agent for you, looking out for his client even when she's dead. But not a lot we can do there. What else?"

"It's a bit indelicate."

"This whole business is indelicate. C'mon, give."

"It looks like Miriam Hopkins and Mrs. Marshall are no big fans of yours."

"No, probably not," she said with a turn of the head.

"Don't be so coy. It's none of my business but word's got around about you and Herbert. By the way, speaking of Miriam and Herbert, well, there's talk."

"Yes. I've heard that talk. You think Miriam or Herbert's wife is behind these threats?"

"Possible. The thread that runs through them is you get out of *Trouble in Paradise*."

"Well, they can just forget it. This is going to be a great film and I'm not going anywhere. Besides which, the studio would never let me out of the picture at this point."

"The source of the threats probably doesn't worry about contractual niceties."

"You've got a point."

"Speaking of the film, it looks like Ernst had a dalliance with the Leena Sparkle girl. Met her at out of the way places: bars, coffee shops, sleazy hotels. He wanted to keep it pretty dark. Oh, and this too. My sources downtown at central precinct tell me his alibi the night of the murder doesn't sound airtight. But genuine alibis seldom do. Looks like he was with another protégé who wants to keep a low profile and he can't find any other witnesses who saw him at the witching hour."

She scratched her head. "I don't quite understand. It's no secret he likes the ladies. Anyway, are you saying Ernst is responsible for the girl's death?"

"Not necessarily. But as the man said, where there's smoke there's fire, and this Leena Sparkle may have had other admirers and detractors at the studio as well."

CHAPTER 17 : DIARY FOR A STAR

Kay opened the door and let in a now familiar visitor. "René, darling, thank you for coming over on such short notice."

"Of course, my dearest love. You sounded so worried on the phone." His calm, soothing tones belied the urgency of his words.

"Truly you're an angel from heaven. Well, something has happened, and I need your help desperately."

"What's that, my sweet?"

"You see, one of my diaries has disappeared, the one for the first half of this year. You remember, I read some of the entries to you."

"Very much so."

"They contain my innermost thoughts, but that's not the important part?"

"What is the important part?"

"It's this: they also mention, sometimes by name, my most intimate contacts, often in colorful language.

In a word, they talk of my lovers. The when, where, even how sometimes. Oh René, if these ever become public … " Her voice quivered with imploring tension.

He stroked her hair gently. "There, there, I'm sure we can figure it out. But who would do such a thing? And why?"

"Those are the questions, aren't they?"

"And how would the thief get access?"

"I keep them in this special hidden compartment here in the bedroom. You remember." She opened the sliding doors and showed him the hidden shelves where the diaries were kept.

"The maid or cleaning ladies?"

"No, that's not possible. Lupe's loyalty is absolute. And I'm sure the cleaning ladies don't even know the diaries exist."

"Have you told the police?"

A decisive shake of the head in the negative. "Good heavens no. The fewer people who know about this the better. News can get around when the police are involved."

"Understood."

"That's why I told you straight away, dear René. You're the only one I can trust."

A gentle clasp of the hand. "May I always be worthy of that trust, my darling."

She looked away as if in thought. "It must have been at the garden party. But these were my friends and colleagues. However – those security guards. They just plain looked suspicious. Do you suppose – "

"Anything's possible. Some of those detective types have pretty rough backgrounds. And they know how to get 'round otherwise secure areas."

"That also makes me think the theft of diaries could have something to do with the girl's murder."

"In what way?"

"I'm not sure. It's just that someone has been sending me these threatening messages that demand I leave *Trouble in Paradise.* Is this a way to get more leverage? Is there a connection with the dead girl? Am I the real target of the murderer?"

"All possible, certainly. Or perhaps the theft is for more traditional reasons."

"You mean blackmail."

"Quite. Has anybody contacted you demanding payment?"

"Nothing yet. And that's what bothers me. All the silence and uncertainty. I don't know what to make of it."

"Precisely. Well, how can I help, my dearest?"

"Start with the detective agency, discreetly mind you. Find out about the men who were here for the party, their backgrounds, character and such."

"Of course, my dear. Immediately. We have a lifetime ahead of us, my sweet. Weeks, months, years. And something like a diary isn't going to interfere with our happiness. We'll find it, I promise you."

"Dear René, such an angel you are."

He got up and walked across the room. She stopped him at the door.

"And René."

"Yes, my darling."

"Be careful." She planted a brief but firm kiss on his lips.

A reassuring smile, then, "Of course I'll be careful."

CHAPTER 18 : PANIC IN PARADISE

The tricky prosperity-is-just-around-the-corner scene now complete, staff and actors were busy preparing themselves for the next take.

Lubitsch began by speaking to his leading lady with his usual combination of concentration and matter-of-factness. "Now Kay, in this next scene – "

The first shot tore through the tall lamp near where she was standing. The glass burst and a couple of people nearby looked in the direction of the lamp. Otherwise no one took any special notice of the mild disturbance. But a security guard recognized the tell-tale sound and said in a booming voice: "Everybody to the floor! That was a gunshot!"

Lubitsch and his crew went to the floor amid much scurrying and random screams.

The second shot hit the mirror just behind Kay, creating a small entry hole but leaving the glass intact.

"Kay, get down or behind something," the guard shouted. "The shooter's aiming at you!"

She neither hid nor went to the ground but stood

tall and upright in a defiant pose. "Where did that shot come from?" she said. "Show yourself, coward!"

Just then the auxiliary door slammed and there was the sound of footsteps running up the stairs. One of the tech staff bolted through the door in an attempt to follow but returned soon after, breathing heavily, saying he was too late and didn't see anyone.

When it was evident the danger had passed a pale Lubitsch picked himself up from the floor. His crew and the rest of the staff followed in turn. Everyone was looking at each other as if awaiting instructions.

"Maybe we call the police?" Lubitsch said, his words coated with an uncharacteristic lilt of uncertainty.

"I guess we do," answered the guard.

As was the norm for him, Inspector Fallon looked dour and serious. He stood up and began to address the small group of people crowded into the spacious but not overly pretentious office. Detective Sergeant Archer sat to Fallon's left.

Also present were Paramount security chief Dixon Peele and his assistant Frank Lugg, Kay Francis, Nelson Charalambides, Gordon Shellhammer and his protégé Miss Dravago, Byron Cato of the actor's union, head of production Al Kaufman, and assistant director Wilson Bromley sitting in for Ernst Lubitsch.

Peele and Lugg sat to the right of Fallon. They were silent and unsmiling. Peele looked like he'd just swallowed a rat and Lugg had a glare in his eyes that said he was ready to tear into both Fallon and Archer any minute but he behaved himself as he sat in his chair in a tense posture.

Most of the attendees had already lit up cigarettes and were puffing away. The exceptions were Dixon Peele and Byron Cato, although Cato nursed a small glass of liquid. A shroud of gently floating smoke rested on a cushion of air up near the ceiling.

Fallon began, "Mr. Janis has requested this meeting and my superiors have designated me as head of investigation. Many thanks to all of you for your attendance on such short notice. And my appreciation to Mr. Peele and the studio for providing this office as a meeting place." Peele managed the barest nod of acknowledgment.

Fallon continued: "I think we'll agree that dramatic measures have to be taken in view of the events of the past few days and in particular the criminal attack this morning. I note with approval that studio management has taken extra measures, most notable being the hiring of additional guards from the Pinkerton Agency. They'll be uniformed as well as plain clothed and will be deployed round the clock in all the buildings in the compound, not just this set.

"Both the police and Paramount have offered Miss Francis protection during her time away from the set but she has declined and said she'll make her own arrangements. Reluctantly we bow to her wishes, though in the case of studio security I wouldn't say it's any great loss for her to be without their company."

"What's that supposed to mean?" Peele growled.

"It means you folks have been asleep at the wheel. One murder has taken place right under your noses. Then this latest attempt just when you're supposed to be on your toes. That's why it's all been turned over to LAPD so the professionals can handle it."

"Go to hell, jerk."

Shellhammer quickly stepped in as front office mouthpiece-in-chief. "All right, Peele, you've had your say. Now calm down. As for you, Lieutenant, could you keep the editorial comments to yourself and get back on track."

Fallon's response was to stare at Shellhammer. An awkward silence filled the room.

"Will the projects continue on schedule?" Cato asked in a meek voice.

"Peele, could you help us out with that question?" Fallon said.

"You're asking my opinion?"

"Yeah, we're asking your opinion. Could you get on with it?"

"Okay, here's what we're going to do. Management insists that the shooting of *Trouble in Paradise* and the smaller projects continue on schedule, and that we'll not give in to this would-be assassin. I'm sure we'll all agree it's a matter of pride and dignity."

"That's great to hear. This fellow's not going to intimidate us," Shellhammer added in grim support while Miss Dravago dutifully nodded.

"Thank you, Gordon," Peele said. "It seems obvious our perpetrator had to have help from the inside to get that close to the set. I'm confident the detective will agree with us there."

"I not only agree, but it brings up all sorts of troubling questions. How did the shooter get into such a controlled area? Why wasn't he recognized? How did it happen there was made-to-order escape route waiting for him?"

With a deep breath Peele said, "We've been through all this before. We've checked all the keys and locks, and all have been accounted for. Furthermore, we've verified that only people who were cleared had access to the set."

"Okay, I think we've expressed our positions," Shellhammer said. "Could we proceed, Dixon?"

"Moreover, we're going through the personnel records of everyone who was anywhere near the set that day. We're also interviewing the same individuals. No exceptions."

"Glad to hear it, Peele," Fallon said. "Those bullets came close, too close. Our preliminary ballistics report suggests the shots were fired by a Smith and Wesson 30, a logical choice for a professional assassin. No one remembers hearing gunfire so we assume our man used a silencer."

Charalambides chimed in with: "Do we know for sure the shooter's motives?"

"Good question," noted Fallon. "It's early, but the growing evidence implies Miss Francis is the real target and the girl's death of a few days ago was a senseless mistake. There's no evidence to suggest anyone else is the mark, though we can't completely rule it out.

"To answer your question: No, we don't know the motive. Is he a pro or a local crazy? An obsessed fan? Who is his employer? Does he have an employer? Were the shots just a warning? Did the same man who shot at Miss Francis drive the car that ran over Miss Sparkle?

"Luckily, we got a break: a witness saw a man exit the auxiliary stars and run out toward the main studio entrance. Then he disappeared. The witness didn't get a look at the man's face, but he was described as slim, wiry, medium height, about thirty years of age and wearing black gloves and a brown hat pulled down to partially obscure his face."

"That narrows it down to half a million men in Southern California," Lugg said. "We've practically got the noose around his neck."

Fallon looked straight at Lugg and said coldly, "Wise-ass remarks aren't going to get us anywhere, tough guy."

"You're the one who wants to play the tough guy, fella."

"All right, Lugg. Take it easy," Shellhammer said as he fidgeted in his chair, small drops of sweat appearing on his forehead.

"Sure, I'll take it easy," Lugg sniffed.

"What's your opinion, Miss Francis? You're keeping awfully silent under the circumstances," Fallon said.

"Um? Oh, I'm just listening. You guys are the experts. But I do have to agree that everything implies I'm the real target."

"Anybody else have something to offer?" An uncomfortable silence answered Fallon's question. "Well, if there's nothing else – "

Shellhammer offered a conciliatory, "Thank you, Lieutenant, and thank you all for your kind attention. Despite the, shall we say, artistic differences, I can say with assurance that we are all on the same page. We'll get this assassin yet."

An hour later Kay entered the bland, one-story

shoebox-like structure which housed Paramount's four screening rooms. Number Four, at twenty seats arranged in the style of a tiny theater, was the smallest and most spartan. She'd chosen it for privacy and access. She walked to the front row and sat down next to Powell, who was already in the room.

"I heard about the events yesterday," he said. "Yes, word does travel fast. A good idea, our little get-together."

She related the meeting she'd just had with the police and security.

"Interesting," he said. "But we might have caught a break, something they didn't mention in the meeting."

"What kind of break?"

"It seems our friends the Lieutenant and detective Sergeant are playing their cards pretty close to the vest."

"Tell me something I don't know."

"Here's something I do know. I've a contact at the downtown precinct. A little encouragement got him to tell me some things."

"I don't care how you did it. Just tell me what you found out."

Powell lit a cigarette and Kay followed suit. Powell said, "Our two friends from LAPD had some luck in their sweep of the studio. They came across this vagrant, who turns out lived at the studio, incognito, real down-on-his-luck type, smell of alcohol all over him. Anyway the night the girl was run down he was sleeping nearby. The sound of a car rumbling by woke him up. He only remembers seeing a large black car through the fog. And no, he didn't see the driver."

Kay's eyes widened. "What else?"

"From the description of the car and what they've been able to piece together from fragments of the tire impressions, they've pegged the vehicle as a late model DeSoto, or Cadillac, probably a coupe in either case. They aren't one hundred per cent certain but it's their best bet."

"That's great work, Bill. I do owe you plenty."

"Forget it."

She looked away for a second, then said, "It doesn't help us with the shooter part, but may yield something later."

Powell exhaled then studiously eyed the lighted end of his cigarette. "You're right. As more things unravel, the puzzle pieces may fit together. By the way, brave of you to turn down the watchdogs."

"Thanks. But what with your assistance and that of my new … secretary, who is close by these days, I think I can handle it."

"Quite the intrepid girl, aren't we?"

"Maybe, but I'm not convinced I'm in real danger."

"How that?"

"It's this: the failed assassination, near miss, whatever you want to call it, has professional written all over it. And since the guy was a pro he must have missed on purpose. There's also the slight chance Ernst or someone else was the target. As usual the police like the obvious explanation."

"Which is?"

"That it was a legitimate murder attempt and the shooter was aiming for me. What gets my back up is: whoever's responsible, they think all this business with the messages and the missed shots will intimidate me. They better think again."

"Well spoken."

"Call it the proverbial hunch, my woman's intuition if you like, but something tells me when you play the hand that's dealt, the wrong person ends up losing the pot, and there's something wrong about the cards in this hand."

"Whatever you say, but I'm not totally convinced."

"In fairness to the police, they usually get it right, and it's possible they have it right this time. But I'm not so sure."

"Okay, I'm listening."

"Basically I think they've got the right shoe on the wrong foot."

"In what way?"

"In assuming I'm the target of these attacks."

"But that's a logical conclusion, to assume you're the target."

"Logical, but not necessarily correct. I suspect the explanation may be elsewhere."

"Then why take all the risk to enter the set, then fire and miss? A warning?"

"More likely a feint."

"A feint? Two shots that miss? Surely you're joking."

"Not at all. The question is: what was the feint trying to obscure? Here's what I think. The girl was the real target all along, for reasons we still don't know. She had to be silenced or made an example of, or both. And you can be sure it had something to do with Paramount. Also organized crime per her visits to Big Eddie's. My guess is the shots at me were more of an afterthought. Besides, if a professional got that close, surely he wouldn't have missed if he were really aiming at me."

"Kay, I admire your imagination, but it sounds a bit far-fetched," Powell said flatly.

"Maybe, maybe not. By the way, this was delivered this morning." She handed a telegram to Powell, who examined it with a quizzical look.

Next time I won't miss. – Avenger

"You call this a feint too?" he said as he gave the telegram back to her.

"I'm not calling it anything. And don't tell the police or security about it. I'm not showing it to them, not just yet. It'll only encourage them."

CHAPTER 19 : LOOKING FOR LOVE

She was pleased to hear the familiar voice at the other end of the phone.

"Kay, dear, I got your message just in time. I'm about to travel to South America. Rio, then Buenos Aires. Tomorrow in fact."

"Thanks much for calling, Nora. I just have to tell someone about ... and you're my best friend."

"What is it you have to tell me about?"

"It's ... a new interest."

"Kay, that's nothing new." A long breath, then, "All right, what's his name?"

"René."

"Oooo. How romantic. Well?"

"It's not that I haven't had lovers before. How does that song say it: have I the right hunch or have I the wrong? It's the uncertainty. I've gotten it wrong so many times with men. You know, happy in love, unhappy in marriage." Her words rolled out fast and agitated.

"Present marriage, perhaps? It's not any of my business, but – "

"You're right. It's not any of your business."

"Now Kay, don't get snippety. Tell me about this René fellow. Who is he anyway?"

"You're starting to sound like my lawyer. They're naturally suspicious types. But I prefer to be trusting, at least until events prove otherwise. Anyway you should understand the workings of the heart. After all, you're such an expert."

"I'm not sure that's the case. But what about your new beau?"

"Oh, he's so much more than a beau. He has a *je ne sais quoi*, so polite and sensitive to my every need. Yes, a good suitor but a darn good secretary too. Mysterious, secretive. You know how men want to be complex. But that's part of the attraction, right? He's an artiste too, screenwriter and does a little acting. Most of all, he has the heart of an artist. And a wonderful amateur piano player. He plays the most romantic ballads for me, right here in my living room on the Baldwin. Sometimes I lie beneath the piano and just … take it. But I do ramble on."

"Ramble you do. He sounds too good to be true."

"He positively is. Not too good to be true, that is. Oh, you know what I mean."

"My thoughts, for what they're worth: is it another fancy of yours, not worth thinking of?"

"Or is it at long last love?" A deep breath. "I go with love for now."

"Tell me more. What does he look like?"

"Just a dream. Late twenties at most. Tall, tan. Ramon Novarro without the mustache, and more masculine. He must have lots of girlfriends. But I don't care. I just don't want to know about them." A pause.

"But then again – "

"Yes?"

"It sounds silly, but I'm afraid I may be too old for him."

"Nonsense. It sounds to me like he's quite smitten. However – and not to rub it in, dear, but by your own admission your record with men is not exactly stellar. And your tendency to fall head over heels – "

"Now you're talking like my lawyer again. But I know what you're saying: unhappy wife, happier lover, sometimes anyway. It's just, this seems different."

"They all seem different at first. But no matter. I must say, this René, he's certainly made an impression on you. And I just have to ask, dearest, how is he – "

"Oh, you mean that. Perfectly wonderful. So attentive and thoughtful, like he is in everything else. He sends me a dozen red roses every day without fail, some days even additional floral arrangements, all charged to me of course but who cares? They all come with the most romantic notes. The feeling is much like the role I'm playing now, you know, Madame Colet. She's wise and tough, but vulnerable too. She's basically a creature of feeling, just wants love and to be loved. I do go on and on, don't I?"

"Kay, dear, I don't mean to be throwing cold water on your party, but do you think it's appropriate for him to send you flowers in his capacity as an employee, then charge the flowers to you? Oh, just a minute – "

She heard Nora's voice in the distance. "Not there, Dorie. Over by the stairs."

"Sorry for the interruption. Last minute preparations. The maid, she doesn't always get it right. So tell me more."

"Well, the more is a rather delicate matter. And you're not to breath a word of it, to anyone."

"Well, what is it I'm not to breath a word of?"

"It's just this. René has been such an angel, agreeing to take on these extra secretarial duties. This is in addition to his own screenwriting and acting career. A true *deus ex machina*, he is."

"Don't overdo it. But what is it I can do to help?"

"Well, inevitably René's artistic endeavors have suffered, and you could help in an indirect way. Specifically, could you ask around? You have lots of contacts. Find a nice screenwriting job for him, or some acting parts?"

"Why me, Kay? You have more influence than I."

"Oh no, that won't do at all. He'd never accept what might seem like charity. If he ever found out … He's very proud, you know. It would be too much for his male vanity. No, no, no. You have contacts too and a nice, subtle way of doing things."

"From what I hear it sounds like he wants you to believe he'll do anything for you, taking on all this extra stuff and such. What's he up to? What is his racket anyway?"

"I don't believe he has a racket."

A deep breath, then, "I suppose I'm the naturally suspicious type, like your lawyers. Well, how can I talk him up if I don't know anything about him? What's he done? Can you send me something he's written? Never mind, I don't have time. Ship sails tomorrow. I'll see what I can do. But I can't promise a lot. I'm on a tight schedule."

"Such a dear you are, Nora."

"I'll be in touch."

CHAPTER 20 : VISIT TO YARRA GLEN

Green rolling hills and swaths of ocean punctuated the views on the drive out to Pacific Palisades. Otherwise the scenery was sparse and empty, the occasional exceptions being the solitary orange stand, gas station, run down diner, or sleazy hamburger joint decorated in the style of an Arabian Nights palace. But still the drive made for a nice distraction from the city and all its complications.

Powell and Kay had exhausted talking about developments in the case and thus the conversation turned predictably to studio gossip, then to even smaller small talk. In a change of pace she said, "Why aren't you telling me where we're going?"

"It's a surprise. Trust me, it could be useful."

Gradually the highway narrowed and the cars were fewer. A solitary lonely house up on the hill would come into view then pass by. Finally the car approached the twelve feet high iron gates, above which a sign in soft pink lettering proclaimed 'YARRA GLEN, Peace from

Illusion,' below which, in smaller letters, was etched 'Claire Amthor, facilitator & proprietor'.

The car stopped and an attendant greeted them. He said he'd have to check with the office. Purely a formality, he insisted, as he went into a booth and made a phone call.

While they were waiting Kay said, "I've heard of this place. Bill, why did you take us on this silly goose chase?"

"That's why I didn't tell you where we were going. I knew you'd disapprove."

"Disapprove? That's an understatement. Shyster psychiatrists, phony spiritualists, self-styled prophets. They're all over the place out here in Los Angeles, leeching people for money."

"But as I said, it could be useful."

A deep breath and a shake of the head in the negative. "Oh Bill, Bill. Since we're here, explain to me how you arrived at your high opinion of this ... whatever it is."

"Don't ask."

"Well, I'm asking. C'mon, let's have it."

"You won't like it."

"I already don't like it. Out with it already."

"I heard about it from my bookie, Niles Oppenheimer."

"Your bookie? You're telling me you brought me all the way out here to see a quack psychic on the recommendation of a bookie?"

"That's exactly what I'm telling you. And I didn't say she's a quack." Powell handed her a card. "Here's the lady's bonafides."

She eyed the card warily. "Claire Amthor, Life Consultant? Oh, please. Why doesn't she just drop the consultant bit and pencil in Delphic Oracle?"

"A little patience, Kay. Have an open mind. This woman has helped the police before and has gotten some interesting results, but they don't like to advertise it. The image of self-sufficiency and all that."

She folded her arms and said, "Whatever you say."

The attendant motioned them to enter. The car meandered through the curvy driveway which wound through a richly manicured lawn. The sprinkling of palm trees along the way provided a nice touch of elegance. A cloying fragrance of mimosa hung over all, blending in strangely with the expected scents of orange blossoms and honeysuckle. The huge Tudor Revival style stone house beckoned as they left the car and walked up toward the large front door.

A rather sinister looking woman dressed all in black, presumably the housekeeper, answered the door. She eyed them suspiciously as they introduced themselves. She nodded and said in clipped words, "Right this way." The woman led them into a huge reception room, whereupon she took her leave. The furnishings oozed all the expected West Country trappings, and Kay commented it could pass for a gothic movie set. Powell agreed.

Then in walked the lady herself, a woman of indeterminate age, Amazonian, nearly six feet tall, quite striking in a hard sort of way with a chalky face devoid of makeup. She looked the part in her Greek style dark grey one-piece which suggested the high priestess.

She approached them and extended her hands. "Hello, I'm Claire Amthor." Her manner seemed warm and she spoke with a pleasing, well modulated mid-Atlantic accent. Her dark, deep set eyes seldom blinked, but instead focused on the person she was talking to. She tilted her head slightly as she listened, as in the manner of an important person giving audience with infinite indulgence and patience.

"Pleased to meet you," said Powel. Kay managed only a nod, unsmiling.

"I received your telegram, Mr. Powell, telling of the particulars of your visit. Thank you for your consideration."

Powell glanced sideways at Kay as he said: "Not at all, not at all."

"Yes, I'm familiar with the story, at least somewhat. Very sad, such a young woman, and such a needless death."

"Yes, indeed," Powell said. "But we should tell you right away that we know of your brother's, um, similar activities. And frankly we're a little … how does one say?"

"Half brother, actually," Miss Amthor said coldly. She quickly returned to form with a congenial, "Skeptical is what you wanted to say, Mr. Powell? It's quite all right, fairly common for first time visitors. As for Julian he has our father's charm and his mother's ruthlessness. And he plays it for all it's worth, literally."

"I take it you have no great regard for him," Powell said. "But one must admit he has quite the following."

"I'd describe them as the needy beau monde rich, well intentioned but vulnerable and so gullible."

"Yes, we were just talking about that," Powell said meekly with a quick glance at Kay.

"Quite. Our place, on the other hand, is where the weary can rest on their life journey and revive their spirits, and bodies. We think of ourselves more as a hotel, the difference being we don't charge for our services; we're supported strictly by our guests' donations and the generosity of foundations and the like." Miss Amthor's careful words flowed like a deep, reassuring river with an inexhaustible source.

"Most noble," Kay quipped.

"I see your friend has her doubts."

"Speaking of doubts," Kay said, "The name Yarra Glen, it's familiar."

"Very perceptive of you, my dear. Of course the name's familiar. It's a small town in Victoria, Australia. The home of Nellie Melba, among its other distinctions. We're not above appropriating a name for the right resonance. I like the sound of it. Yarra Glen. So soft, so calm." She looked out the huge window in the direction of the ocean as she lovingly spoke the words. "Seems to fit the mood here, in our, shall we say, kingdom by the sea."

Kay looked at Powell unsmiling.

"Yes, we noticed that on the drive over here," he said.

Miss Amthor continued, "As I was saying, guests here have a range of opportunities for working through their challenges, both in groups and individually. Moreover, inasmuch as we are a center for healing that goes beyond the purely physical, we also have recreational and artistic activities. And sometimes I give private consultations where I call on my powers to commune with the world beyond this one. This gives much comfort to troubled individuals, also grieving family members and such."

Kay rolled her eyes and she looked upward.

As if sensing the need for a change in the conversation, their hostess offered a curt, "But enough with the talk. Shall we go back to the sanctum?"

"Sanctum. Right," Powell said.

They all left the main drawing room and walked slowly down a long stone corridor with no pictures on the walls. Soothing strains of low volume classical music wafted from an unseen source.

They made their way to a spacious, high-ceilinged, sparsely furnished room. At the far end sat an ornate oak desk. The high window behind it proclaimed a certain importance to the space, the lady's personal office no doubt. A davenport backed up against the far wall, and one large painting, that of a striking woman rendered in the American Impressionist style, rested above the huge fireplace at the opposite wall.

"Beautiful portrait. Lovely woman," Kay said.

"Thanks. It's my mother. They tell me I inherited my intellectual bent from her. That and my spiritual powers."

Miss Amthor motioned invitingly with her hands toward the oval shaped table discreetly located near the fireplace and away from the desk. "Sit down and get comfortable," she said. Then she lit two candles, closed the curtains, shut off all remaining lights and joined them at the table.

"Aren't we supposed to hold hands or something?" Kay asked.

"No, my dear. Nothing quite so melodramatic. Sorry to disappoint."

After everyone had a moment to settle in, Miss Amthor instructed all to close their eyes. She extended the palms of her hands outward and rested them on the table, after which bowed her head down and took in a few deep breaths. For a minute or two she was silent and didn't move.

With her eyes still closed, she slowly pulled her head upright began to speak. Her delivery changed to a kind of Continental accent with upper crust British overtones. "Oh, benevolent forces of light, we call upon you, join us. Reveal your secrets to those of us in this world of illusion, so we may release this child from her torment and uncertainty in her journey. Also we ask that you provide guidance to those present in their quest for a worldly justice." Her head went down to the table and she quivered a bit. Her eyes still closed, she brought her head back up.

Her facial muscles tightened as she began to speak.

"I see … pictures, yes … flickering images. Black and white forms, well-dressed people, some sort of formal affair. Now an audience: it seems far away, far away in time. Chairs, like a classroom. Someone is speaking. He says 'masterpiece, the great man's touch, yes, it's there'."

She paused and took in a few more breaths, slower, deeper. "Now the images … less clear. Fog, and greys. Money in a thin envelope. Small, no, large bills. A beautiful young woman, stylish clothes, French clothes. A sweet but troubled girl. And yes, also a man, tall, rugged, a teacher, or helper, thick hair, his, no, the girl's perhaps. And dancing." She shook her head back and forth in a motion suggesting intense concentration, then she continued, "Some kind of club, lots of smoke, liquor, colorful people, music, Latin music. But also shouts, arguments, gunfire. Blue colors, clothes, perhaps, men and women, no, just men wearing blue, powder blue, or navy blue."

Miss Amthor jerked her head in a spasmodic movement and her hands clenched. Her face and voice tightened and she spoke with an American accent. The voice quivered with a painful quality. "Please, help me … I'm between worlds … so confusing. I want to get this all behind me. But I can't proceed, as long as – "

A silence. Miss Amthor weaved and rocked back and forth a few times in a slow movement. She returned to her own soft voice. "Tell us, my child, what must be resolved and how can it be done?"

Miss Amthor's head tilted sharply to the left and the girl's voice returned. "You can't make me do this! I'm going to be a great actress. I won't be part of your schemes and trickery! No … the fog, footsteps. The car. No! No!"

Claire Amthor threw back her head and led out a kind of ecstatic shriek. Her body trembled and went rigid in an epileptic apotheosis. A few seconds later her head, arms and upper body collapsed onto the table.

The dramatic events at Yarra Glen dominated the conversation during the drive back to the city. Kay remained unconvinced. "Illuminating, certainly theatrical, but not necessarily other worldly. Most of what she said could be verified through reading the papers. That and a couple of phone calls to the right people. She had plenty of time to concoct a vision for her communication with the beyond."

Powell jumped in: "But you've got to admit her performance was impressive. She sure gave us our money's worth."

"That's the whole point. She doesn't charge. You get what you pay for."

Powell countered, "Well, when we slipped a hundred dollars into the donation tray on the way out she didn't complain. Speaking of money, the bit about the cash in envelopes is interesting."

"Bill, don't be naïve. Money's behind everything in the movie business, behind everything in crime. In our whole culture. No points for her there; she's got to do better than that."

"She did catch the girl's accent. Remember, she moved from Columbus, Ohio, as a teenager."

"So what? Lots of people out here speak with a Midwestern accent."

"And the part about the blue clothes. And the black and white flickering images. Fascinating stuff."

"Blues, reds, black and whites, off-grey, powder white, flickering. Who cares? She's just throwing in a little spice, sprinkling in details like glitter to distract us and keep everything a touch mysterious."

"But how about the girl's Paris chic clothes? That's not come out. I barely know it myself and only because I had a good look in her apartment."

"That's true, but probably just a lucky guess. Lots of actresses wear Paris fashions. But in any case hardly conclusive, and what does it reveal about what it's all about and who's behind it?"

"Curious she didn't say anything about the shots that missed."

"It probably just means she concentrated on the dead girl. Made-to-order Leena Sparkle was, for all those beautiful phony trances and hysterical, from-the-beyond messages. I'll say this for Miss Amthor: she's one good actress."

"We can agree on that." Powell took in and, let out a long breath. "A frustrating day."

"But not a total waste. Who knows? Maybe I'll go back and stay at Miss Amthor's … hotel, when my spirit needs a little cleansing and renewal. A nice metaphysical bubble bath, just the thing."

"Sounds like an idea. But why do I get the feeling you're protesting a little too much."

"Maybe because I am."

"Well?"

"It's nothing very specific. But there were some things she said that were … interesting. By the way, did you notice the grey Plymouth behind us that's been there all day?"

"I hadn't noticed."

"That's the same kind of car studio security would drive. And I told them I didn't want their coddling. Do you suppose they're tailing us on the sly?"

"Can't say. But I know all the studios are pretty jealous about protecting their property."

"That's the part I don't like."

"That they're overly protective of you?"

"No. What I object to is they think I'm their property."

CHAPTER 21 : STEAK OUT
WITH JOEY CHICAGO

Kay's pale blue limousine lurked outside along the curb, looking a bit out of place amidst the black Plymouths and Buicks. The driver waited patiently as he read a copy of *True Romances* magazine.

So this was the place where Joey wanted to meet? Kay walked to the entrance of the *Tahitian Bar & Grill* and skeptically eyed the bright pink neon sign overhead. She opened the door, entered and glanced over at the cocktail bar behind a bamboo curtain.

A delicate looking man with bouffant hair slumped languorously at a Chickering baby grand. He was dressed in a cheap tux sporting a blue carnation, and a thin cigarette drooped from the side of his mouth. He had a tired, far off look in his eyes as he caressed the piano suggestively, his long, soft fingers barely touching the keys. He puckered his lips in a kind of kiss of recognition as he saw her. He'd been playing a Latin tune she didn't recognize but upon seeing her launched into "I'll Build a Stairway to Paradise," singing in a voice a half tone flat and playing in a limp that stumbled every other step on his trek heavenward.

She listened for a few seconds, nodded to the man and entered the main restaurant. Along the way she pulled out a dollar bill and instructed to maître to put the money in the pianist's brandy snifter.

She eyed Joey at a table in the corner and strolled over toward him.

Joey promptly arose upon Kay's presence and greeted her politely but cautiously. They sat down and Joey began, "Thanks for coming over."

"My pleasure. Very interesting place," Kay said as she scanned the main dining room.

"Terrible music, sorry."

Kay shook her head. "No problem. I hear the food's pretty good."

"Yeah, the scenery too," Joey said as he nodded in the direction of the fleshy blonde waitress who was strolling over to their table. "Say, I'm kinda hungry. Okay if I order some dinner?"

"Sure, but I'll just have coffee."

The waitress gave them menus, and Joey studied both the menu and the blonde. He settled for steak and eggs. "More of a breakfast meal, but it's what I fancy right now," he offered in way of apology.

"It's all right. Don't worry. I'm still buying." Kay said. "Just coffee for me."

The waitress scribbled down the order as she munched gum and eyed Joey warily. She then sashayed away, Joey's eyes in tow.

"Window shopper?"

He laughed and waved a dismissive hand.

"Why did you pick this place?" Kay said.

"As you say, the food is good. Other reasons too," he said with a glance back at the waitress.

"So what have you got for me?"

"I found out about the man the girl had the argument with. It took some askin' around but I got it. His name's Frank Quinn, a policemen. He comes to Big Eddie's every now and then, official or unofficial, who knows, but always dressed in civilian clothes. Doesn't advertise he's a cop, behaves himself real good."

"I appreciate your efforts, Joey."

"Thanks. Anyhow this Quinn guy, he has the rank of Lieutenant at the main station downtown, fairly high up, works in the office, paper shufflin' or somethin'. Definitely not a beat cop. Nobody gets too excited about him comin' to Eddie's, you know, what with the word out Prohibition's days are numbered, cops get more casual about showin' themselves in places like Eddie's."

"It does make you wonder why they even bothered in the first place."

"A lot of the folks I associate with wonder just the same thing. Anyhow this Quinn fella likes to hang out in the main room but sometimes goes in the back and plays poker. He specially likes to chum around with Sheldon LaSalle and Fergus Chilk. They're Eddie's glorified bookkeepers. They called themselves accountants. He likes to visit their offices and talk with them."

"The poker he played, was it for high stakes?"

"Are you kidding me? From what I heard his limit to bet was singles, sometimes not even that. I think he just liked the company, the relaxation, whatever."

"Who's this Chilk and LaSalle. Shady characters?"

Joey shook his head in the negative. "Pretty straight arrows. They were real accountants in another life and started workin' at Eddie's because the pay was better plus a few extra goodies. Access to girls, the occasional free bottle of good wine, that sorta thing."

"Well, that rules out high level gambling debts for explaining our mystery man."

"I guess so. Big Eddie's gets all kinds, so an ordinary lookin' guy like Quinn don't specially stand out. Eddie's kinda' proud about it, the clientele. Blackmailers, shyster lawyers, legit lawyers, crooked D.A.'s, politicians' wives, rough cops, bored cops, horny cops, straight cops that can be oiled but aren't all bad. Racketeers, pornographers, quack doctors, slick gamblers a little too slick for their own good, they all come in."

"Okay, Joey. You made your point. By the way, did a bookie named Oppenheimer ever show up there?"

"Can't say one way or the other. I don't know everything goes on. What about this Oppenheimer?"

"I know him in another context. I just wondered if he fit in here."

"I guess not."

"How about a woman named Amthor? Tall, sort of British, aristocratic."

"Never heard of her. Is she important?"

Kay looked away. "No, not really. Let's get back to the girl."

"Like I said before, I didn't know the girl. I just observed. That's my specialty, seein' and hearin'."

"So let's have it. What have you seen and heard?"

The waitress brought Joey's dinner and Kay's

coffee. Joey tore right into his steak as he kept talking "She always presented herself nice, a classy dresser, but liked the drink a little too much and she would get to talkin'."

Joey paused to take a swig of his Coca-Cola to wash down the food. "This Coke needs some rum to get it up on its feet. Too bad they don't serve alcohol in here."

"Refreshing to see some people really take the law seriously."

"Yeah, but about the girl, as I says somehow she knew this Quinn guy but mostly she was with the natty lookin' dressers, maybe gangsters, maybe studio executives. Tell you the truth I can't much tell the difference. One's as good as the other. Same faces, expressions, manner, especially the clothes. All full of themselves, tryin' to prove they're sharper than the other guy, hoping their own high opinion of themselves will rub off on the competitors and enemies.

"But mostly they wanna impress the dames so they act important and throw around lots of money. To me it's all the rackets and one big con job. No offense, miss, but the movies ain't high art."

Kay sipped her coffee and allowed herself a sly smile. The piano player in the lounge launched into a bluesy arrangement of "Mood Indigo," which despite the missed notes and slowish tempos glided pleasingly through the muffled clutter of sounds.

Joey took another swig of his Coke. "If you ask me they're all people who've been waitin' at the stop sign of life, lookin' in both directions for the big break, like the has-been prize fighter who's one punch away from the title fight. That's the problem; they'll always be that one punch away. What they don't see is the fix is in."

"I like you, Joey. You're a stand up-guy with resources and good insight. May I ask you a personal question?"

Joey sat up straight and placed both his hands on the table. "Sure. Fire away."

"Your … line of work. What is it that – "

"You mean why do I do what I do? It's because it makes me feel really alive, sometimes anyway, and important after a fashion. Gives me that extra charge. Do you know what I mean? They say the same thing about the straight cops, the private dicks too. Beats sleepwalkin' through life the way so many folks do these days."

"You're quite a philosopher."

"My friends peg me as a thinker," he said as he wolfed down his eggs in one gulp. He got out a cigarette, lit it and offered one to Kay, but she declined. He took a long puff, blew out the smoke and said, "How do you like that? A thinking man's wise guy." He let out one of his patented giggles.

"Think about this." She placed two one hundred dollar bills on his side of the table. "A retainer plus a bonus for your good work so far."

Joey's eyes widened as he leaned forward and looked at the money.

She then slid a large manila envelope across the table. "I've got some more work for you. It's all in there. Fifty dollars a day plus expenses. There'll be more bonuses for you, depending on what you find."

Joey beamed a wide smile. "You got it."

The cheerful law office receptionist recognized her voice right away and put her through to Gerald Fiedler.

"Gerald, Kay."

"My dear Kay. Always a pleasure. How can I be of service?"

"I've an unusual request."

"Usual, unusual. We aim to please."

"Well, here it is. Have your snoops talk to Beckwith & Torquin. They're the folks who audit Paramount's books every year. Grease whatever palms are necessary but find out where the money goes."

"Where the money goes?" Fiedler's well pronounced words projected an unctuous incredulity.

"That's right. But not the usual stuff you can find in a glossy annual report, which just lists things like production and distribution costs, stars' salaries, publicity."

"What else is there?"

"What I want is anything that smells funny. Unaccounted for funds, hidden books, a minor star whose salary is way too big. Be sure to check on the girl who was murdered and see if her salary squares with the going rates. And, no, I won't tell you my reasons. Only that I'm doing a little … research on my own, and it may have something to do with financial irregularities at Paramount. And that it's important to me."

"An unorthodox request, my dear Kay, but certainly feasible. I must say that you insure that life at this office will never be dull."

"Gerald, you say all the right things."

"But that's my job, to say the right things."

"Quite so. many thanks. We'll be in touch."

CHAPTER 22 : HOLDING MISS WALSH'S HAND

The two smartly dressed women nursed their coffees in the cozy, well-appointed French restaurant as violin and piano music gently hummed in the background.

The younger woman let out a leisurely sigh, followed with: "Such a beautiful place. And I'm so honored to meet you, Miss Francis."

"Please, it's Kay."

"Then you must call me Connie."

A nod and smile. "A deal."

"That music they're playing. It's so lovely. What is it?"

"Delibes' Flower Duet from *Lakmé*."

"It's utterly beautiful. And I'm impressed with your knowledge."

"Oh, thank you."

The waiter brought them a tray of desserts then scurried away. Both Kay and Connie went for the Russian tea cookies. Kay sipped on her coffee while Connie enjoyed her Earl Grey. The music changed to the Meditation from *Thaïs*.

Kay leaned forward as she addressed her youthful companion. "Miss Walsh ... Connie. Thanks so much for seeing me. And excuse me for getting right to the point. I told you some of the particulars over the phone, but it's this: Bill and I heard about the police interviewing you to confirm Ernst's alibi, and that you were reticent. I can understand, but we need your help, just to verify who's a real suspect and who's not."

Connie looked away and hesitated. "Those policeman weren't very nice, you know. And those awful rooms they talk to you in. I just told them I didn't know anything, that Mr. Lubitsch must have been mistaken. I guess I fibbed a little but I just don't want to get involved."

"Yes. I understand. The police can be very insistent and not so subtle."

"I asked a lawyer friend of mine and he said I didn't have to say anything because I'm not under subpoena and I'm not a suspect or accessory. Anyhow as I said I just don't want to get involved. For private reasons." She munched on her cookie and had another sip of tea.

"Jealous boyfriend?"

She turned away. "Something like that."

"Connie, I don't mean to pry. Whatever your reasons are – " Connie maintained a wary silence as Kay sipped her coffee. "It's just, if we can absolutely rule out Mr. Lubitsch as a suspect then our job is easier in finding the girl's true murderer. And I'll be very grateful."

Kay reached across the table and gave Connie's hand a comforting squeeze. Kay held the hand a couple of seconds and then let go. To her surprise Connie grabbed her hand right back and looked directly into her eyes as if she was gauging Kay's sincerity or trustworthiness. *Poor girl. Just nerves. Needs lots of reassuring.*

Finally Connie let go of the hand. "You'll not say anything?" Her voice was soft.

Sensing an encouraging lilt in the question, Kay quickly responded. "Of course not."

"Well, there was this event at the Roosevelt Hotel. That night all of us were in the dining room and our tables were close together. This rather distinguished looking gentleman, he asks me to dance." She had a sip of tea and made a quick scan of the restaurant.

Sensing a need to fill in the silence, Kay offered, "Yes, he has quite the eye for the ladies."

"Anyway I explained I was a model and a dancer just starting out and that I was attending a local models' convention. So we talked a bit. While dancing he told me who he was. I think he wanted to flirt but I wasn't very responsive. But all the same he said he'd be there a couple of days and told me to stop by his suite and see him if I'd like. The next day the convention was over and afterward there was a social with dancing and such and at about ten o'clock I called him from the lobby phone and asked if I could come up to his room. He seemed very pleased to hear from me.

"When I entered his suite he was wearing some kind of smoking jacket or robe. He looked real happy to see me. I put my coat on the large sofa and asked him if I could go into the bath, and when I got there I noticed all sorts of exotic ladies' perfumes and sprays, set out on the mantle, which I thought was strange."

"Strange … why?"

"All those products, for a man? I didn't get it. Anyway I go into the bath then return a few minutes later and explained to him all the ladies' rooms downstairs were taken or out of order and I had kind of an emergency and I was sure he wouldn't mind my using the bath in his room. I thanked him and put on my jacket and started to leave. Funny, he seemed kind of shocked: he had a strange look on his face as I left the room. I noticed a bellman there at the door with lots of caviar and roses, also a bottle of champagne. It looked like Mr. Lubitsch was expecting company."

"Yes, it sure sounds like he was."

"I suppose. Whatever you say. As I told you I didn't want to talk to the policemen. An official record of me being in his room at that hour and all that. I just didn't want to give an impression I was his girl."

"Yes, I understand. He probably wanted to give that impression. Anyhow we'll be discreet and the police won't have to know. And you don't have to talk to them if you don't want to. Meanwhile I'll see what I can do for you at Paramount."

They wound down the conversation with film industry small talk as they finished their desserts. As both stood up to say their goodbyes, Connie offered, "Oh, thank you, Miss Francis, you're a wonderful person."

Kay raised a mock admonishing finger.

"All right. I mean Kay. And you're still wonderful." With a forward thrust she draped her arms around Kay and pressed the full frame of her body up against her. The two women locked in a tight embrace and Connie planted a moist kiss flush on Kay's lips. She held the hug and kiss a little longer than the usual Hollywood air kiss. Kay felt her body getting warm as her face turned a couple shades of pink. The hint of desire hung over the two women like a cloud of cheap aftershave.

Then Connie finally let her loose with a gushing, "Thank you, thank you." She looked straight into Kay's eyes and smiled as she said the words, then left the restaurant.

Still a bit flustered, Kay tended to the bill then asked if she could use the office phone to which the restaurant manager happily obliged.

"Hello Bill. Kay here. Not exactly big news but I wanted to update you. We can cross Ernst off our list as a legitimate suspect. It looks like his story checks out, sort of."

Amid interspersed chuckles from Powell, she explained in summary version the girl's comedy of errors. Then she continued, "It was ten o'clock or so when Leena Sparkle was run over, so Ernst couldn't have done it. But he wanted to play it as some kind of big seduction scene in his hotel room. Funny how he didn't mention the bellman, who could have verified his whereabouts just as well. The problem was the girl didn't play along. Anyhow he was never a realistic candidate. But his would-be girlfriend is a little more … interesting."

"Right you are," Powell said. "But at least it makes our job a little easier. So Ernst's pride was ruffled? Par for the course. Despite his reputation for a roving eye old Ernst never had much luck with the ladies, at least that's what I've heard. Great story though. Good material for one of my comedies."

"Well, in this case Ernst never had a chance from

the start. The girl doesn't exactly have an eye for the men, if you get my drift."

"I … get your drift."

CHAPTER 23 : BAD FORTUNE AT THE HOUSE OF BAMBOO

Jimmy's House of Bamboo was packed as usual. It wasn't the cheapest Chinese in town but the food was great and the place had an unsavory aura from its location in the heart of Chinatown, which only added to the appeal. One could even glimpse a film star there on occasion though none was present that afternoon.

Jimmy insisted he descended from a long line of obscure Chinese emperors. He didn't seem to mind that few took the claim seriously. In any case it didn't keep the folks from showing up en masse for the sumptuous cuisine.

The tinkling of glasses and silverware at midday accompanied the low rumble obbligato of the myriad conversations, one an unlikely trio of customers crowded into a booth on the far rim of the restaurant.

"Carlotta Von Teese. I like the sound of it. Is that your real name?" Sergeant Archer's question suggested his interest went beyond the purely professional.

Carlotta was a striking woman of middle years who wore a purple sequin dress, fox fur coat and pull down hat. Inspector Fallon rested his jaw on the palm of his hand as he looked on and listened.

"Silly boy," the lady answered. "Of course not. I thought it fit the part better than Blanche Mecklenburg, which is what I went by back in Indianapolis." Carlotta spoke with an affected upper class accent that disguised her obscure pedigree.

Archer's eyes squinted and his face mock grimaced. "Ouch. You said it." He took a swig of water and inhaled deeply on his cigarette. "Off the record – " He hesitated, scratched his head, then said, "Carlotta, or is it Blanche?"

"Please, Carlotta," she said with best flirtatious smile and tilt of the head. "But just call me Lotta. That's what my friends, close friends, call me." She reached across the table and gave his hand a gentle squeeze, then withdrew her hand.

Lieutenant Fallon observed all with patience and curiosity. When a cop works with another cop for four years he learns a few things about him, and he knew his junior partner liked the ladies and probably visited houses the type of which Carlotta ran. But this kind of attentiveness was a bit much. Fallon took in and let out a long breath loud enough for his companions to hear.

Unfazed by his partner's apparent disapproval, Archer continued, "Well, Lotta, as I was saying – " His eyes darted quickly in his partner's direction, then returned to Lotta. "And this is not necessarily what I think, but some would say yours is an honorable profession, almost a public service. All done in a free market sort of way. Very American."

Fallon jumped in: "That's only one opinion, Archer. Some of us have real girlfriends and their public service is quite sufficient, thank you."

Duly chastised but still in amicable mode, Archer smiled and touched his fingers to his forehead in the manner of a salute.

Lotta smiled and let out a deep sigh. "Ah, girlfriends. The bane of so many honest working girls these days. But I thank you all the same for the compliment, Sergeant. The police aren't always so … professionally understanding." She glanced at Fallon as she said the words.

Just then a waiter appeared carrying two large plates of appetizers. He placed them on the table then quietly disappeared.

"But what can I do for you boys? You didn't invite me to Jimmy's to debate the merits of the oldest profession." She scooped some appetizers onto her small dish as she spoke.

Fallon began, "You're right. Now, Carlotta … "

"Why don't you call me Lotta, like your friend does?"

"I'll stick with Carlotta if you don't mind. And he's not my friend; he's my partner."

She shrugged.

"Which brings me to the purpose of our visit. We've gotten a tip that you might be able to help us out. Tell you the truth I'm skeptical, but our source insisted and he's what we call usually reliable."

"Sounds exciting."

"Furthermore, your place over on Wilshire, the police higher ups give it a pass due to an accommodation on your part, and I make no criticism of their judgment. I just follow the drift. Anyway we're here today for another reason, to investigate one murder and a second attempted murder."

"You put it so delicately, Lieutenant. I don't give the police an accommodation. It's called a discount. And by the way my establishment isn't a place. It has a name, in fact it's had several names. A few years ago it was called the Plazuela Arms Apartments. Quite genteel, don't you think? But now I dub it Lotta Von Teese's Land of Smiles, like the operetta. Classy."

Fallon tried to get back on course. "Okay, okay, we didn't come here to get a dissertation. We want to know if you've heard anything about the death of the actress Leena Sparkle, also the shots that were fired at Kay Francis and missed."

"Oh, my powers of observation are much over-rated, I'm sure," she said with a glance upward. She then threw herself into a second helping of appetizers, scraping generous portions onto her plate. Her rough-edged table manners made that of the two cops seem dainty.

Fallon nodded to Archer, who clasped Carlotta's hand gently and placed a twenty dollar bill in it. Then he withdrew the hand. She stuffed the bill down the top of her dress then got back to the appetizers.

Fallon pressed her, "C'mon Carlotta, throw us some gossip. Let me help you out. Here's some gossip: we've heard the stories about how the best wines, champagne, caviar and cold cuts magically appear in the drawing room when the vice squad shows up at your house - on a token raid, of course - then afterwards you look the other way when they sit themselves down and enjoy the hospitality. Yeah, we have sources too."

"Mutually looking the other way," she said. "How very democratic. Does it have a double meaning? But those stories are so exaggerated. What's your source? *The Times*? But now that you mention it – " She patted her chest where she'd put the twenty dollar bill. "My memory is improving."

Fallon nodded to Archer, who slipped her a second twenty.

She accepted the tribute and tucked it away in the same place. "Well, the mind is beginning to focus."

"Here comes Jimmy," Archer said.

"Right on time as always," Fallon huffed.

Dressed in black tux, Jimmy Wong strolled over to their table. His round, well scrubbed face and broad, toothy smile spoke of much self-satisfaction.

The two men arose, said hello, shook hands with Jimmy and sat back down.

Jimmy remained standing and said, "I see you're having Jimmy's Signature Special appetizers. My own, personal secret recipe. I'm rather proud of it." Jimmy spoke in respectable English laced with heavy Chinese accent.

"Tastes great as always, Jimmy," Archer said.

"You honor me with your praise, Sergeant. It is always reassuring to have the company of the finest of Los Angeles." He bowed and they returned the gesture, more in the way of nods.

"And of course a woman of Miss Von Teese's caliber is always welcome. She truly graces us with her serene presence."

"Oh Jimmy, you're such a flatterer. But I'll take the compliment all the same," she said with primp of the hair. "I don't believe I've ever been called serene."

"Quite appropriate for a true lady like yourself. And, may I say, I'm so happy to see that a good restaurant makes for, what is the phrase, strange bedfellows. But I leave you all to enjoy our gracious food, the surroundings and your own company." Jimmy bowed once more then crept away.

"Jimmy's looking prosperous these days," Lotta said.

Fallon's rejoinder was less sanguine. "He's a little too smooth for me. And I've got a feeling his prosperity doesn't derive totally from legit means. By the way you didn't hear that."

Lotta gave a nod but seemed absorbed in a table across the room at which sat two snappily dressed men and a rather elegantly attired woman. Lotta waved and blew a kiss to the woman, who returned the wave but not the kiss.

"Friend of yours?" Fallon said.

"You don't recognize her? Oh, I bet your partner does."

Archer shrugged and shook his head in the negative.

"Well, she's Luanne Treadwell. She runs the House of Mirth over on Figueroa."

"Professional acquaintance?"

'Quite. She's well thought of in the business. But I'm afraid I don't recognize the two gentlemen."

"We can help you out there, and they aren't gentlemen. One is Johnny Rosso and the other Vinny Lambino, mid-level mob figures out here. We've had our encounters with them."

"I must say I'm impressed."

"Yeah." Fallon struck a match with his thumbnail then lit his cigarette. "But why is she here with them acting so cozy?"

"Search me," Lotta protested. "Maybe she just likes their company."

"Right. But getting back to our conversation … "

Lotta took the hint. "Yes, naturally I've heard of both the incidents to which you refer. I read the papers too. I take it the trail has gone cold and you boys are, as they say, leaving no stone unturned. Word was the deceased lady was quite the party girl. As for the shooting we presume it was done by a pro, not somebody who worked on the set."

"Yeah, yeah, we know all about that. What else?"

"Well, everybody noticed the girl lived an elegant lifestyle for a B actress. She either had support from another source or a second line of work."

"Like your line of work?"

"Could be."

"Well, did she?"

"Did she what?"

"Work at your place?"

"Of course not. But there was one of our girls – "

"One of your girls?"

"Yes. Paulette Noire was her name, her professional name anyway. She doesn't work for us anymore. She and this Leena Sparkle were friends. They both studied at a so-called acting school over on Olvera Street. Paulette said she never knew anyone with such drive. And fussy about her men – " Lotta took another bite of her shrimp appetizer. "She said the girl told her she could only love a handsome man and would only let a rich man make love to her."

133

"Interesting. Anything more?"

"Something Paulette said struck me, and that was the girl fancied herself an intellectual. She so wanted to be heard and wanted to talk about ideas. But nobody, especially the men, paid her any matter. They were too busy looking at her clothes, imagining her unclothed, noticing the way she crossed and uncrossed her legs, put her hands on her hips and tossed her head back at an angle."

"We hadn't heard the part about wanting to be a thinker. Well, was she?"

"Was she what?"

"An intellectual."

"How would I know? I never met her. What I heard was she was quite the glamour girl and everybody responded to the looks."

"Yeah, we know that part. Kay Francis lookalike and all that. What else?"

"Nothing else. Paulette wasn't the sentimental type. When she got the bad news she just shrugged and went about her business. In our profession life always goes on."

"In ours too. Did Paulette mention anything about boyfriends, anybody special on the set, actors, technical people, writers?"

"She didn't say anything to me about it. And she certainly would have; we like to talk among ourselves. But you've got to remember Paulette knew the girl before she became ... well, at least a minor star."

"Anything else?"

Lotta placed the palms of her hands on the table and she sat more upright. "I thought that was plenty."

Just then the waiter appeared, precariously balancing four steaming entrées with his arm cocked beneath his shoulder. He placed the large, heaping dishes on their table then scurried away. Lotta eyed the food with keen anticipation.

Fallon, Archer and Lotta settled in for a leisurely lunch which included much small talk. Both detectives attempted, in ways subtle and not so subtle, to pry out of Carlotta the identities of her clientele, male and female. But, distracted by all the food, Carlotta's memory was fading, and besides, clients were a locked door she never opened to outsiders.

CHAPTER 24 : DRIZZLY AND OVERCAST BUT HOPING FOR SUNSHINE

Drizzling rain in the grey evening twilight provided an apt counterpoint for the tiny café. In a corner booth Archer and Fallon swilled their stale coffee.

"Do you get the feeling she's holding out on us?" Archer said.

"Sure. She knows something. The question is: what is it, and why the closed mouth? Lotta's usually more talkative."

"Now you're calling her Lotta."

"It suits her. I just didn't want to give her the satisfaction. By the way, what was that infatuated fan business about? For real or just to get on her good side?"

"A little bit of both maybe," Archer said. "What do you make of the folks upstairs and their hot tip that she might know something?"

Fallon's response was a grunt that hinted of a chuckle. "I don't know. You know how they're so tight-lipped about their so-called sources."

"But she doesn't have to be so mum. She could have greased us for more favors," Archer said.

"I smell other interests involved. One of her high-powered clients, maybe even a cop. Either way somebody put the gag on her."

Archer lit a cigarette. "Not much action either from that tail we put on Powell and the princess. A tough case to crack."

Fallon exhaled a wheeze of a breath. "Film business cases are always tough. What do we have then? Not one of our more memorable days. A madam who won't talk, and a meet cute with a high priestess out in Pacific Palisades."

"Maybe Kay Francis thinks the woman will surround her with a little angel glow, to scare the bad guys away, like crucifixes and vampires."

"You're a real wit, Archer." Fallon made a face as he sipped his coffee.

"You think she and Powell are tying to freelance this thing?"

Fallon shook his head sidewise. "Don't even know that for sure. After the visit to the psychic, and probably unbeknownst to Powell, she has dinner with a shady character at a sleazy diner. What's that about? I don't get it."

"Could be what she's doing has no connection with the dead girl or the shots that were fired."

"It's possible. But I'm not buying. Anyway we've had some good and not-so-good leads and just don't have the resources to follow up all of them. And whatever she's up to it's not worth the energy and expense of surveillance. We'll keep the tail but just for a couple more days and that's all. If this so called assassin's after her he sure hasn't made his move yet. Bottom line: following her isn't getting us anywhere. We got more out of Lotta."

"Funny how Lotta only fed us stuff we already know. The girl lived the good life, the clothes, riding club and so on, source of her funds unknown. Even the part about her actress friend didn't help us any."

"It sure didn't. But Lotta knew plenty about the girl from a second-hand source. It doesn't quite square with me."

"Maybe she knows something that could hang a pinch on someone. Someone she wants to protect."

"I figure if she's covering, her reasons for doing so aren't totally noble."

"Payoff?"

"Sure. Anyhow I suspect Lotta has a pipeline of her own, all the way down to the precinct. Getting back to the girl, as far as we can figure she was smart and paid everything with cash, and had plenty of cash to throw around."

"Sugar daddy?"

"Maybe. Probably. But nobody at the studio's talking. The parents neither, said they didn't know of any special boyfriend. Speaking of Paramount, you can be sure the security people know stuff they aren't telling us."

"That Lugg fellow is a real pain in the ass."

"That's why we went to Lotta in the first place. We know the stars, execs, staff, anyone who can afford the bill, goes to Lotta's and similar places. She's a better source than the people at the studio except she's not singing."

"Sure isn't."

Fallon tapped his pencil on the counter and scratched his eyebrows. "Interesting how the brass isn't pushing us on this one. It's like they want it to die a natural death."

"Funny business?"

"Maybe. Funny or no, I'm with them. God, this case is giving me a headache. And this isn't helping a bit." He gulped one more swig of his coffee and threw the paper cup into a nearby trash container.

"Awful stuff."

"The real connection, the only thing in common, is the studio. It's got to be. The girl worked there. Kay Francis works there. The car ran down the girl on the studio lot. The shots were fired on the set."

"And the threatening telegrams, they're all ultimatums to get Kay Francis to leave the picture."

"Check. But a movie studio like Paramount, it's a big place. It's like saying two crimes are connected because they both happened in Los Angeles County. Tell you the truth, I'm ready to cold case this one any minute."

The well coiffed woman walked through the hotel lobby and proceeded directly to the toll phone. She inserted a nickel and dialed the number that had been given her.

"Hello, it's me."

"Are you using the right phone?"

"Of course I'm using the right phone, just as you said. Why the mystery? And who is this?"

"Never mind who this is. Let's just say I have the studio's best interests at heart." The words at the other end of the phone glided off the tongue in well-massaged style.

"All right. Have it your way. By the way I just loved Jimmy's culinary wonders. The moo goo gai pan was simply sublime, the best I've had this side of Singapore."

"You've been to Singapore?"

"Oops, I let it slip out. But I figure my secret's safe with you. I thought a Midwestern background was more to the point than Singapore Annie. That might attract attention. Anyhow there are so many Midwesterners out here nobody gives a second thought when I tell them I'm a Hoosier at heart."

"Okay, I'm impressed with your credentials. What did the two policemen tell you?"

"Not very much actually. They don't know anything; they're just chasing their tails. I gave them a song and dance about the actress and her friend who worked at my place, part true, part made up and part what I knew already. They found it interesting but not that useful. Tell you the truth I think they're getting pretty frustrated."

"That's good news. But I hear Kay Francis is doing a little snooping around on her own. Did the police say anything about that?"

"No, nothing. They didn't talk about her."

"Maybe they don't know."

"As I told you, they don't seem to know much. By the way, that well-placed tip they got about me being a good source. Did you have anything to do with that?"

"Never mind about that. What else did you find out?"

"Oh, I thought you might be interested: I got an extra bonus for you."

"What's that?"

"I saw a colleague and she happened to be dining with underworld figures. The two police gentlemen knew them and they took an interest."

"Great work. It'll keep them off balance while we work on the powers to lay off and let things simmer down. Meanwhile we'll continue to express our appreciation for your efforts. You got the last delivery?"

"Yes, I got the last delivery. And I get the message. You scratch my back, I'll scratch your back."

"Dearest Lotta. Never let it be said you mince words. You're doing a great service to the studio and we all know what's good for the studio is good for America."

"Bravely spoken."

"Best not to let something like this get out of hand. People might interpret things the wrong way, and that would be … inconvenient. Thanks, Lotta. You know we won't forget this."

"I won't let you forget it. By the way say hello to the missus."

A silence. Then a forced chortle, "If only I could. Talk to you later."

CHAPTER 25 : SAM'S USED CARS
AND GETAWAY VEHICLES

Joey and his traveling companion stopped at the Elite Diner just outside the Glendale city limits. Joey told his friend the meal was on his star client, but professional ethics didn't allow him to reveal the identity. His friend seemed suitably impressed and in any case enjoyed the free meal.

Joey spent a little time chinning the fleshy, redheaded waitress. He told her she looked just like Ruth Chatterton and she responded with a huge smile. Joey explained that he and his pal were having trouble finding Sam's Used Cars, and she took the time to methodically give him precise directions. Since he wasn't paying, Joey took the attentive admirer role a step further by leaving an absurdly large tip for the girl as he left.

The oversize, nondescript sign out front blared "Sam's Used Cars – Every Day a Bargain." Joey drove into a spacious lot filled with all types of cars, also a few trucks, and he and his hulking companion got out of the car and walked toward the tiny shack that passed for an office.

The faded white paint on the outside was peeling, like the tanned, sun-dried face of an aging movie queen. Like the aging actress the structure more or less got the job done but without much style.

They went inside and there at the small desk sat a man of about forty, short, sweaty, and fifty pounds overweight with a three days old silver stubble of a beard. He wore thick round glasses and chomped on an unlit cigar at the side of his mouth.

"You Sam?" Joey said.

"Yeah, I'm Sam. What can I do ya' for?"

"It's more like what we can do you for. Oh, by the way, I'm Joey Chicago and this here is my associate Frank "Fitzie" Fitzsimmons."

Sam's smile disappeared as he eyed both men warily.

"But they call me Frankie the Fist for short." Joey's mountain of a companion spoke his words in a smoky, gravelly voice. "Like my more famous pugilistic namesake." Frankie raised his right hand, made a fist and stabbed a couple of mock punches in the air.

"Pugil what?" Sam said.

Joey intervened with: "Okay, so we know you had a DeSoto here a couple of weeks ago. We read the ad in the paper but don't see it now."

As Joey spoke Sam's face turned a few shades of pale, then he said, "Uh, I'm not sure actually."

"Quit the stall. We just want to know a little information. Mostly, who did you sell it to?"

With voice a pitch higher Sam managed an unsteady, "I … don't really remember. I'd have to check my books."

Joey gave a nod to Frankie the Fist, who delivered a swift backhand blow across Sam's face. The force of Frankie's gigantic hand sent Sam to the ground.

"That's just a warning," Joey said. "A sample, would we say."

Sam was shaking and could barely get the words out as he climbed up to his desk and sat down. Blood started to drip from his lower lip. "Okay, this guy, tough, serious, looked like a football payer, he came here, bought the DeSoto. Paid cash, more than he needed to pay. Then he gave me an extra five hundred dollars to skip the paperwork and forget I ever sold him the car."

Joey flashed a thin smile then through his trademark giggle said, "That's better. Now just one other thing." Joey handed Sam four photos. "Look at these. Recognize any of 'em?"

After looking at the third photo Sam said, "Yeah, that's him. That's the guy that bought the car."

"Positive?"

"Positive. No doubt about it."

"Yeah, he's a rough character. We sorta know him. But we've got a better offer for you: we'll let you breathe. And keep all you teeth. Comprende?"

"Yeah, comprende," Sam said with a tight, painful smile.

"But – " Joey added, waiving his finger. "No talk about our visit."

"Or you'll see us again. And I won't go so easy on ya." Frankie the Fist's admonition was somewhat unnecessary but Sam's nod said he got the message all the same.

CHAPTER 26 : GOSSIPING WITH PRUNELLA

Kay had other things to do at seven on Saturday morning but thought she'd better respond to such a summons. Her mood was upbeat but pensive as she sat on the little bench atop the south-facing slope of Mount Hollywood. The high fog was beginning to set in and the soupy air and accompanying smells and sounds gave the scene a strangely primeval quality. The low sun strained to peek through the jungle of trees up on the hills. A hint of light mist gave the park and the surrounding houses perched up on the hill a velvety glow. She breathed in the cool, moist air with a voracious gulp and noticed a touch of honeysuckle and jacaranda mixed in amongst the other seductive fragrances.

However pleasant the setting, it made for an unlikely meeting place with the most widely read, and feared, gossip columnist in all of Los Angeles. What the devil did Prunella Holloway want at such an unruly hour? Did she have a hot tip about the girl's murder?

Prunella had her sources official and otherwise, mostly otherwise, but the notion that she might have a handle on the murder was an unlikely prospect at best. Kay never saw the lady socially. She hadn't invited her to the garden party, a slight Prunella wouldn't take umbrage to. For someone like her to attend such an event, peppered with stars and film industry types, especially in the wake-like circumstances, would be the proverbial mixture of oil and water.

Kay's musings were interrupted as she caught Prunella's visage in the distance. Prunella Holloway was an overripe woman of fiftyish years and she walked up the hill with a lilt that belied her generous frame. Today she wore a nice two-piece business suit that looked a little warm in the friendly weather. She carried herself with impeccable posture and generally classy air but as she got nearer Kay noticed she wore a little too much rouge and makeup.

"Kay, darling, good to see you again."

"Likewise, I'm sure, Prunella."

They greeted each other with a handclasp and air kisses but both ladies' stiff posture and the hint of tension in their voices suggested wariness.

"Lovely setting," Prunella said. "It's where I like to come to ponder."

Kay often wondered about Prunella's snooty upper crust accent but she always kept her curiosity to herself, sufficing with: "Well, what is it you want to ponder today?"

Prunella flashed a knowing smile. "My darling Kay, that's what I love about you. No nonsense. You come right to the point. And you don't mind hiding your impatience, even with me."

"Thanks. You're pretty direct too. Anyhow you were talking about coming to the point?"

"Of course, my love. But I must tell you: I heard of your garden party, even the juicy bit about the good doctor falling asleep, also Noel Coward's visit. And, slightly scandalous of you, letting that bête noir herself Louise Brooks attend. Oh, and not least of all, I got the scoop about your new, um, secretary. One woman said to me, word for word, cross my heart: 'he says he's her secretary, she says he's her secretary, maybe he really is her secretary'. Don't worry, my dear, I'm not going to print it any of it."

"Well, print it if you want! And let them say what they will. He's a lovely man and a fine secretary."

"Yes, I'm sure he is, on both counts."

"Anyway, I don't want to debate the merits of my new secretary."

"Indeed not, my dear. Well, where to begin? May as well just plain say it."

"Say what?"

"I know about the missing diary."

Kay's face turned a couple shades of pale which gave her dusky complexion a not unattractive ivory patina. "How do you know of it? And what do you know of it?" Kay shook her head back and forth quickly. "Anyway, why should I care?"

"First, never mind how I know, I just know. And I can only presume somebody probably wants something in return for seeing it gets back to you."

"Then how – "

"As I just said … Oh, never mind." Prunella flashed a knowing smile, then: "As for why you should care, my dear, I not only know about it being stolen, I've seen it, actually read some passages. And they are, well, un poco spicy. I must say after your description of the encounter with that assistant director I needed to take a cold shower – or two."

"I guess you have me then."

"Don't worry; I won't go public with it. And let me assure you, my love, the contents are in, shall we say, a safe place. We've always gotten along, Kay. And you know I've never printed something about you I couldn't verify. And believe me, I've heard things, but I hear things about many stars and much of it never makes its way into print."

"Most kind and appreciated." Kay's voice turned into a near whisper. "Well, what do you want from me?"

"Nothing."

"Nothing? You have me meet you here at this filthy hour to tell me you've seen the diary and want nothing."

"That's right, nothing. Not now, anyway. Just someday when I need a favor from you … And besides, contrary to popular opinion, I do have a heart. And I may just be concerned and trying to do you a good turn."

"That's fair enough. You've got a deal. But what can you tell me about the diary?"

"As I said I can't tell you anything."

"You had to find out somehow. Was it the thief trying to shake you down for a juicy story? He wanted to sell the story for money, that's it."

Prunella shook her head in the negative.

Kay pressed on. "Just tell me this? Does the stolen diary have anything to do with the girl's murder?"

"I don't know if it has anything to do with the girl's murder. Or anything else for that matter. All I can tell you is I did find out … something, and somehow, and yes, I managed to read a few passages. But I can't go around revealing sources."

"Oh, Pru. You and your sources."

"My dearest, sources are the oxygen of a gossip's pathetic existence. I'm sure you understand."

"I'm not sure I do understand."

"No, I didn't think you would. By the way I notice you're not wearing your wedding ring. Is there anything you want to tell me? Something for my column? I've heard a few rumblings."

"No, nothing to tell you. Read the papers."

"Dear Kay, ever the private person."

"As are you, Prunella."

With a tilt back of her head and a spontaneous laugh, Prunella said, "Enough then. I know when I'm licked. Anyway I must toodle. I've a date with a scandal just waiting to happen in a hotel down in the Bunker Hill district."

"One of your sources?"

"How perceptive of you." Prunella started to get up from the bench. "But just one word of advice – "

"What's that?"

"Your new … you call him your secretary: be careful. The same for Herbert's wife. I think she knows of the dalliance. No, I'm not going to print that either. But she's a spiteful woman, could do anything. And about that murder business, too. Have a care."

"Thanks for the caution. I'm always careful."

Prunella nodded, then turned round and walked away.

CHAPTER 27 : THERE'S JUST NO ACCOUNTING FOR TWO SETS OF BOOKS

Lupe answered the phone in her usual businesslike manner. "Miss Francis's residence." She listened, then turned toward the patio and said it a loud voice, "It's Mr. Fielder, ma'am."

Kay put down her cup of coffee and the afternoon paper. "Oh, thanks, Lupe. I'll be right there." She walked quickly into the house while Lupe made herself scarce.

"Kay, It's Gerald."

"Gerald. You're a godsend, just in time."

"Don't overpraise me until you hear what I have to say."

"Okay, I'm ready."

"Per an initial perusal of Paramount's books, compliments of a low grade staff member at Beckwith, everything is in order and the company is downright squeaky clean, officially."

"The officially part sounds interesting."

"Quite. But first, about Miss Sparkle. The past six months her salary has been two hundred fifty dollars a week, which seems a commensurate amount for a second tier, mostly supporting actress."

"Yes, that sounds about right. But you hinted there might be something else."

"Indeed. Our source favored us with further keys to the kingdom, for quite reasonable remunerative considerations all things considered. To be precise, there was a second set of books that contained a more accurate listing of disbursements to show where the money really went."

"Well?"

"Quite. In particular a group of funds that stood out, exactly the type of thing it sounded like you were looking for." Fielder delivered his words in customary well-oiled style.

"Tell me about it."

"It seems there were monies listed under 'discretionary contingency funds', reserved mostly for the front office, ranging in individual amounts from fifteen thousand dollars all the way up to one hundred fifty thousand. It's assumed these funds were distributed in cash, as there's no bank drafts or other physical record."

"Intriguing. Go on."

"It gets better: there's no breakdown on how these monies were spent. And there's no names mentioned, only departments or sections."

"Those are some impressive figures considering there's no accountability. Which departments got the money?"

"Let's see. Oh, yes, here we are. As I said most was

in administration. Then there was security, publicity, production. No actors or anybody else from the artistic side, the only exception being funds set aside for what they called directorial projects. I presume this meant Mr. Lubitsch."

"Yes. He is a rather special case, isn't he? Which department had the largest amount?"

"The Executive Director's, of course."

"After that?"

"After that, just a moment … bear with me … head of production, a couple of Arman Janis's top assistants, then directorial, and brining up the rear, security and legal."

"No huge surprises."

"No, I suppose not. Speaking of surprises, there's more news. Our man on the inside is dangling the promise of even juicier material. Pure dynamite, he calls it. It sounds like he's using it as leverage to get more tribute out of us."

"Sounds like it could be important. What do you think?"

"What he's given us so far has been good, so I'm inclined to believe his story."

"I'd say we need to get it."

"He's demanding a substantial honorarium."

"How much?"

"Five thousand. That's on top of the five we already paid him."

She squinted her eyes and bit her bottom lip. "It's a lot of money. But I need the dynamite. Get it."

"Will do. Now Kay dear, not to be too inquisitive, but could you tell me what this is all about?"

"Sorry. No can do. But if I find what I'm looking

for you'll read about it in the papers."

"Surely you're joking."

"I wish I were. Thanks again, Gerald. I await the good news."

She put down the phone and stared across the lawn. *Why the need for multiple contingency funds? And why take the risk of putting it all down on paper? Couldn't Janis just control all the funds and dole out whatever is needed, whenever needed? Something's not quite right here.*

CHAPTER 28 : LOOKING FOR AN ENDING

On her way to the *Trouble in Paradise* set Kay traversed the enormous maze of a structure that was Stage Four. Sam Raphaelson, looking distracted and intense as usual, almost bumped into her as he scurried round a corner.

"Sam!" she said. "What brings you to the trenches?"

"One or two fine points to discuss with the man."

"Got an ending yet?"

"I'm working on it."

"Make me look good," she said with raised finger.

"I will, but it'll have a twist."

"The best endings always do."

"Anyhow it'll soften the blow for the Code boys and all their delicate sensibilities. They're giving us a hard time over the idea of a pair of high-class thieves not married and living together. We're trying to finesse that and may just get away with it. They also take umbrage at Gaston and Lily getting away scot-free."

"Criminals getting away without punishment. Fancy that."

"Fancy that yourself. We know it never happens in real life, don't we? They're also their having a fit with Charlie's line where he says he likes to take his fun and leave it."

"That's such a great line. Why didn't you give it to Madame Colet? It fits her character so well."

"I give her plenty of good lines."

"Yes you do. Fair enough then. Oh, there's Ernst. I must run now."

CHAPTER 29 : MIRIAM CRASHES THE SET

"I know all your tricks," Marshall whispered in a low murmur.

"And you're going to fall for them."

"You're conceited."

"But attractive …"

"Now let me say – "

"Shut up. Kiss me." Marshall and Kay locked in a passionate embrace as their lips met.

She never tired of rehearsing this scene, a principal reason being Herbert Marshall's luscious enfolding and ensuing kiss. But there was also that wonderful black sequin bias cut tank dress she wore which melted down her elongated torso and showed off her curves so suggestively. It just felt so … good hugging her skin. And that deep décolletage in the front and the back, slightly scandalous but so elegant. The same for the strand of pearls which engulfed her neck and just went on forever. Simply divine.

"Cut! Print. Vonderful job, Herbert, Kay, simply marvelous. Good to be working again and back on track. We'll put all this business behind us and produce a great film. Thanks to you all."

Lubitsch was in buoyant mood, but a voice from offstage intruded on the high spirits. "Bravo! Fabulous! You're right, Ernst. Great job. They did just VONDERFUL." Miriam Hopkins clapped her hands as she slurred the words.

"Careful, she's been drinking," a voice whispered.

"You're damn right I've been drinking." Miriam said as she walked unsteadily onto the set. "That hot kiss was so realistic, you'd just swear they weren't acting. What say you, Herbert? Was that acting? When you told me I was the only one for you, was that acting too?"

Marshall walked over to Miriam, took her hand and put his arm around her shoulder. He spoke in a soft, soothing voice. "Miriam dear, you're not quite yourself. Imagining all these things. Shall we go back to your dressing room?"

Miriam pulled herself away from Marshall's protective embrace. "I'm not going anywhere, except maybe out of this picture." She walked up to Kay and stood a few feet away from her. "Just first let me say a few words to this … man-eater, or do we just plain call you a … No, that's too good for you."

"Miriam, calm down. I think you'd better leave, right now," Kay said.

"You bet I'll leave. I'll leave the whole damn picture! But first a few words of advice for the queen bee."

"Miriam, that's enough. Really." Kay's voice was subdued but insistent as she spoke her words rapidly.

Miriam turned in the direction of Marshall. "Were you ever embraced and kissed by an absolute cad? Well, be sure to shower with hot water afterward – and use lots of scouring powder!" She then faced Kay. "And remember what I told you: either you go or I go!"

Miriam turned away and walked off the set.

After a tense moment of silence a few voices started to mumble and the technical crew continued with their work.

Marshall made a sympathetic gesture with his hand to Kay that signaled he would be with her right away. But first he walked over to Lubitsch.

"You'd better see her soon, old man," he said. "One of your soothing talks."

Lubitsch wiped sweat off his forehead. "Yes, I suppose I'll have to. We can't lose her at this stage in the picture. But let me tell you: such talks are getting more challenging."

"Quite."

"And Herbert, the sooner you learn to control your urges on the set, the better."

"But Ernst, I have a reputation to protect. I'm under strict orders from my agent to appear in the gossip columns as often as possible. Honestly, it's wearing me out. Have a little pity."

"Ah, publicity. Life would be so much easier if these female stars would accept once and for all that it's a man's world and they should be grateful for the little considerations. And anyhow it's just as advantageous for their careers if their names get mentioned in the columns coupled with a major leading man such as you."

Marshall nodded in concurrence and a serious look

crept onto his face. "I promise to behave myself better. An incentive of a sort: with the wife in town I have to be more careful."

"I'm very glad to hear it."

"But still, that womanly pride of Miriam's, ruffled as it is. A difficult thing."

"Difficult woman," Lubitsch said.

CHAPTER 30 : THE MATH ADDS UP

Relaxing in her bungalow dressing room after the tense encounter, Kay inhaled deeply on her cigarette and took another sip of cognac. Just then the telephone tinkled. Its ring was a welcome intrusion.

"Miss Francis?" the operator said.

"Yes?"

"A Mr. Fiedler calling."

"Yes, I'll take the call." She puffed her cigarette as she waited for the call to be transferred.

"Kay. Gerald here."

"Yes, Gerald, give me the good news."

"Well, our friend came through, in a manner of speaking. It seems there's one more ledger, a kind of appendix, eyes only type thing. It includes a rather vague section titled miscellaneous income, presumably some kind of sales, but here's the rub: no sources are cited."

"Why do I smell they're hiding something?"

"Precisely. Well, what's really interesting is the mathematics of the thing. It seems most of the so-called contingency expenses found their way back into said miscellaneous income ledger, dollar for dollar. Right there in the columns and rows. And they all check out, but in rather varying amounts, apparently disguised to make the entries seem more random. As I said most of the money was there."

"You say most of the money. How much didn't make it back?"

"One hundred fifty thousand dollars."

"That's a large amount to overlook."

"Quite."

She turned away from the phone and muttered, "Maybe that's the point. They didn't overlook it."

"What was that? I didn't quite catch it all?"

"Oh, nothing. Many, many thanks. I like this math, because, contrary to the ledger, it all adds up."

"Whatever you say, my dear, but I prefer simple math."

"Well, as the man said, sometimes one plus one gets you two and sometimes it gets you eleven. How's that for simple math? Thanks, Gerald."

CHAPTER 31 : CONFRONTATION IN THE COMMISSARY

They sat in the front row of Screening Room Four. Powell lit a cigarette and took a sip of his brandy. "We've really got to stop meeting like this."

"If all goes well it'll be over soon," Kay said. "And there'll be no more need for meetings."

"Then let's hope all goes well."

Kay lit a cigarette. "Your guy Joey sure came through for us."

"He's a good sort actually. Much more to him than meets the eye. But it stings a bit that you did an end around me and worked with him on your own."

"Sorry Bill, but there was something – I just had to … do it myself. It had to be my show."

"I understand. Also great work by your legal wizard. Thanks for cutting me in on this. Any theories as to the creative math?"

"Several. Well, one in particular. But I'll keep it to myself till I've got something more tangible. Anyway, first things first."

"Right. Speaking of first things first, looks like we've got our guy. And I like your plan."

"But the thing is, we need to go after him right away before he panics and does something stupid, like spraying a few bullets, or worse, leave town. I can't go with you, sorry. I'm tied up all morning with *Trouble in Paradise* rehearsals, important scenes I can't get out of."

"It'll be all right. I told him I needed to see him and talk over some things about the gunshots that came your way, asking for his expertise, you know, flattery and all that."

"Sounds like a good strategy."

"I liked your notion of meeting in a public place, so I sold him on the commissary. I thought that would be unthreatening. The part he doesn't know is that I cajoled a couple of Pinkerton guards, plain-clothes thank you, to keep a watch. But I'm still worried. You're sure it's a good idea not calling in the police or even the security folks?"

"I'm thinking if we bring along the police or Dixon Peele it'll just put him on his guard. This way if you confront him he might tip his hand and let something slip."

"Like who his boss is."

"Precisely. And you already said you've got the guards as muscle. Good luck, Bill. I'll be checking in soon."

The Paramount commissary buzzed with late morning sounds and movements as the tinkling of silverware and voices created a pleasant cacophony. Powell and Lugg sat at a far corner table.

"How's the daughter?" Powell said.

"Fine. Enjoying her first semester at USC Law School." Lugg did his best to affect an indifferent, affable exterior.

"That's good to hear," Powell said. "Good old college days. I remember. I was young once, about a hundred years ago." Powell seemed confident; he'd done this sort of scene before, at least on-screen. He mused that his acting skills came in handy in unlikely places.

Lugg forced a chuckle. "I know what you mean. But you didn't ask me here to talk about university days and my daughter's studies."

"Very astute. When I asked you to meet me I said I wanted to talk over the shots that were fired, which is true, in a roundabout sort of way."

Lugg listened but seemed distracted. He gazed in the direction of the security guards, who sat at the counter trying to look inconspicuous. After glaring at them for a few seconds, he said, "What is it you're getting at?"

"What I'm getting at is this: it's over, Lugg. We know you did it, the girl's murder. As for the stray shots that missed Kay, we know you didn't do that. The shooter was strictly outside talent, a real pro. Besides, we've confirmed you were in another building when it happened and we'll very likely never know who the shooter was. Probably you don't know his identity either. The fewer the better, as the man said. Oh, and this too: in case you wondered why we didn't call in Dixon Peele, we wanted to spare you the embarrassment, for the moment anyway."

"What are you talking about, Powell? Are you nuts or just drunk?"

"I assure you I'm quite sober. By the way I had a chat with the security guard who found the girl's body that night. He said he tried to call you repeatedly at home and your office but couldn't get hold of you. He didn't have Peele's number so he called the LAPD. But somehow you knew to show up just at the moment the cops were arriving on the scene."

"That's easy – "

Powell held up his hand and said, "I knew you'd have a ready explanation. No matter. We've got better goods: the DeSoto that ran her over, we tracked it down. It wasn't easy, mind you. A good job you did hiding your tracks. But we have resources too, and the car finally turned up. We found, well, not the car – we suspect you tore it apart or ditched it in the ocean or burned it or something – but we located the place where you bought it out in Glendale and the guy who sold it to you. He identified you from a photo."

"I don't know what you're talking about." Lugg's face tightened with lines of tension while encroaching perspiration dampened his face. His body assumed a tense posture as though waiting to spring.

Powell continued, "We know you're just muscle. Tell us who hired you and I'm sure the D.A. will go easier on you. If you catch a break it'll be your boss who dances on air and not you. With a good lawyer maybe you can trim it down to, say, twenty years and out in ten. We know your motive: you were desperate for money for your daughter's education. Also you needed money to appease an alimony hungry ex-wife and her attack dog attorney. We found out about that too."

In a quick movement Lugg lurched at Powell and caught him with enough of his forearm to send him flying out of his chair to the floor. Lugg scrambled from the table and headed toward the nearest exit, decking a waitress and sending her tray of food and drinks careening in the process. As he opened the door a shot rang out. Lugg grabbed his shoulder but kept moving. People from the commissary started to scream and scurry about.

"Don't shoot, for Gods sake!" Powell yelled as he got up from the floor. *Well, if I did this in 'The Canary Murder Case' I can do it here.*

Powell exited the building in pursuit of Lugg, the two Pinkerton guards in tow. A troop of extras dressed as Roman soldiers was marching down an open area in between the buildings. Lugg blundered into them and a voice yelled "Cut!" Powell was about fifty feet behind him, the Pinkertons another twenty feet behind Powell.

The Romans hesitated and watched Lugg as he puffed his way round a corner. Powell and the guards did their best to wind their way through the maze of extras, who were looking on with increasing curiosity.

When Powell turned the corner he didn't see Lugg anywhere, but he noticed a nearby open door which led to Stage Three. He entered the gigantic structure, which was bathed in a half-dark twilight.

In the distance Powell noticed the bright set lights which were on and he made his way towards the shoot which was in progress. He saw Lugg, sweating and panting, standing off set among a group of extras looking around warily and holding his shoulder. He stood out like a Siamese cat at a mouse convention.

Powell crept into the light and Lugg spotted him.

Lugg turned to run away but there were too many bodies in his way. He changed directions and stumbled right onto the set.

Victor McLaglen and Richard Arlen were in a sitting room with fireplace and walls lined with books. Arlen had just said, "Now get this straight, detective," as Lugg materialized. He crashed into a wine bar and sent several bottles spilling and breaking wildly. Champagne corks exploded and the bubbling liquid spewed all over Lugg, Arlen, and McLaglen. Lugg bumped into Arlen and tossed him aside. The force sent Arlen to the floor while McLaglen tiptoed in a backward direction.

Meanwhile Powell shoved some bodies and tried to get near the set and Lugg.

"What's going on!" a loud voice blared

"Keep the cameras rolling?" someone shouted.

"Hell yes!" blurted an enthusiastic voice.

Lugg found his way to the edge of the set and ducked behind a large partition.

Powell, now breathing heavily, followed but couldn't find him. Lugg had disappeared. Powell just stood there, a quizzical look on his face.

One of the Pinkerton guards showed up. "Where did he go?"

"Not sure," Powell said as he looked in both directions.

Just then gunfire, two shots in rapid succession. The sounds crackled through the soft darkness and echoed with a mocking insistence.

Kay eagerly awaited the voice at the other end of the phone.

"Powell here."

"Bill! What's going on?"

"You probably heard about my little drama."

"Yes, something about it. Sounds like it was a bit more dramatic for Lugg. What exactly happened?"

"The short version: Lugg panicked during our chat and took it on the lam. He terrified a bunch of people and destroyed a couple of sets along the way. One of the guards wounded him but that was just the beginning of his troubles. Then I lost sight of him. The next thing I knew, two shots and Lugg got it in the head and the heart. Looks like the killer back-windowed it. Not a trace."

"Sounds like the work of a real expert."

"You said it. The scuttlebutt is Lugg died instantly so he didn't make any last minute confessions. But if you ask me he was just the tool, not the real mastermind. I doubt he even knew who his employer was."

"I'm sure that's the case. Who was there just after Lugg bought it?"

"Some B unit staff and extras, Peele and all sorts of security folks, Charalambides, who was just wandering by, then a little later Shellhammer and his Gal Friday."

"No big surprises. By the way, where are you?"

"I'm down at the police station. Your pals Fallon and Archer are beside themselves about why I didn't call them in when I gave Lugg the third degree. They're hinting they may arrest me. Interfering in an investigation, withholding evidence and all sorts of other good stuff."

"Well, let them have their fit. And Bill, a big favor."

"What's that?"

"Sit tight and don't tell the police anything about our adventures. I'm sure the legal boys will be there any minute and fix everything for you."

"Are you kidding? I'm starting to enjoy my visits here."

"Thanks, Bill."

CHAPTER 32 : SHOWDOWN
ON STAGE FOUR

The well modulated voice spoke with oily precision. "Kay, your call is a happy surprise. And at this hour. As they say, to what do I owe the pleasure?"

"Can you meet me at your Stage Four office? Ten-thirty. Sorry for calling this late, but it's important."

"Important is as important does. See you there."

The chauffeur was off that night so she drove the limousine herself to Paramount. She said hello to the guard as she passed through the main gate. He always seemed pleased to see her and he waved her through nonchalantly.

"Working late, Miss Francis?" he said in a snappy voice as she passed.

"Late enough."

She drove over to Stage Four, parked the car and headed towards the huge structure. Everything was silent and near dark when she entered but no matter. She knew the place well enough to find her way around blindfolded. A few of the offices and technical rooms had lights on but by that hour it felt like a lonely place. A few auxiliary lights in the cavernous interior twinkled in a greyish blur. She mused it would have been the perfect ambience for a mystery set in Bloomsbury.

The building was a gigantic barn of a structure that could have passed for an aircraft carrier factory except for the rather haphazardly arranged individual sets. A basketball court here, legal office there. A Dutch windmill gave way to an Aztec temple. Then a Currier and Ives house, complete with picket fence, which in turn metamorphosed into a Western saloon which she recognized as a B effort called *Showdown at Sunset*. She then found herself in a small night club-like interior with its faux touches: Moroccan-style doors, papier-mâché palm trees with stuffed monkeys, fake blue sky and stars, waterfall with de rigueur garish Hawaiian landscape. The last set she passed through was the elaborate Madame Colet Deco house for *Trouble in Paradise* with its elegant winding stairway.

She made her way to a long corridor at the end of the building which led to several small offices. One had a bright light on inside. It made the space stand out among the London fog lighting effects of the stage proper.

The door to the office was unlocked and she let herself in. She poked around the papers on the desk. They were mostly columns of numbers and inter-office memos. She tried the file cabinet drawers but they were all locked. As she began to have another look at the desk she heard the creaking sound of the door opening.

"Looking for something, Kay? Or just here boning up for tomorrow's shoot?"

Gordon Shellhammer had materialized without

warning. He looked his cool, calm, well-dressed self.

"Maybe I'm going for a little extra credit."

He didn't respond to the witticism.

"I'll try again. Yes, Gordon, now that you mention it, I'm looking for something to incriminate you in the deaths of Frank Lugg and Leena Sparkle. But you're a smart guy and wouldn't leave anything lying around, least of all in your office."

Shellhammer managed a labored chuckle. "What a great little kidder you are. This is what you said was so important over the phone?"

"I'm afraid it's no joke."

His smile and affable exterior vanished. "No, not a joke. And I'm not surprised. You always had a serious side."

"There's nothing more serious than murder."

"You're absolutely right. But since you have this imagination, entertain me. Tell me how I'm connected with the girl's murder."

"Not just the girl's murder. Don't forget your muscle man Lugg."

"Oh, sorry. How remiss to overlook, since you flatter me with two murders. But please, continue. I find your digression fascinating."

"It was the money."

"The money?"

"I'll start at the beginning so you can follow. It's now obvious that Leena's murder was staged to make it look like I was the real target. I ruled out a jealous wife. The same for Miriam. She hates me but not enough to commit murder to get me out of the picture. Besides, I just don't see her as having the nerve. Anyway the whole thing was too convoluted for an amateur like a wife or rival actress to pull off.

"So it had to be an inside job, someone with brains and clout. It could have been somebody from the front office, and yes, maybe Charalambides or one of the legal guys. But in one case not enough imagination and in another not enough cheek. But you, Gordon, you're just smart enough, but more important, arrogant enough to think you could get away with it using your position to cover things up."

"You flatter me to imply I have so much clout."

"Oh, it's not flattery. But it is the clout. As they say you're the man who gets things done."

"I try."

"Don't be so modest. Anyway it all fits together so well. Right in front of my eyes but I didn't see it at first."

"What was it that ... clarified your vision?"

"As I said the money. I did a little investigating of Paramount's books, on my own. Very illuminating. All those phony funds, a hundred fifty grand left over. That was your expense account. But management didn't want to get too specific as to who controlled the funds. They just wanted you to handle things ... your way."

"You've done some homework. I'm impressed."

"All that extra money sneaked in with no specific person mentioned, that told me a lot. Only you and maybe someone from the front office knew about it. Doesn't matter who. I'm surprised you didn't do away with him too. Anyway top management wanted absolute deniability of exactly who controlled the money and how it was spent. No tracing of the funds. And you were willing to take the risk for the hefty salary, the perks and the power it gave you. And this too: it was you who sent me all those phony Western Union warnings signed Avenger. How hokey can you get? I figured those were fake from the beginning."

"I never had much flair for drama."

"Oh, I'd say you have quite the flair. Speaking of which, the diary. Was that your idea too?"

"What diary? What are you talking about?"

She wasn't sure why but she tended to believe him. "Oh, never mind. How about getting me a glass of water? All this explanation is making me thirsty."

"Sure. Just don't try anything cute."

He walked over to the corner, filled a paper cup from the water cooler and handed it to her.

"Thanks."

"A pleasure. Go on. This is good."

Kay helped herself to a few sips of water, took in a deep breath and let it out. "It's obvious now that Leena Sparke was the runner who took the payoffs to certain parties so they would look the other way when delicate matters came up with the studio. I suspect others shared in the bounty: the occasional madam, gossip columnist or journalist, troublesome ex-wives, all paid via courier too. But mostly the cash went to certain strategic recipients downtown. That explains how Bill Powell's breaking and entering charge just disappeared."

"Truly fascinating. Continue."

"You paid Leena a bit and she had a token salary as an actress. And Ernst probably gave her some money. She was his girl, did you know?"

Shellhammer's face tightened and his eyes grew bigger as she said the words.

"I can see you didn't. Was she your girl too?

177

Anyway her tastes were a little too elegant and she got the idea to skim some money while doing her courier work, which some people took exception to. This Quinn guy was the enforcer or messenger, whatever. Their very public disagreement at Big Eddie's was the last straw and you knew she had to be silenced, after which you could work on getting back into good graces. Ergo you paid Lugg a tidy amount to run over the girl. He probably never knew who he was working for."

"Quite an imagination you've got. You may have a second career as a screenwriter. But you lack one little detail. Proof."

"Correct. For the moment. But once the police and D.A. start to dig into the front office's books and follow the trail of the money they'll pry out who gave you the cash, and where it went. They're smart guys, the police. You underestimate them."

"It looks like I underestimated you." His voice was thin and bitter.

"And some of them are still straight."

"Some of them?"

"The police. How confusing it'll be when this is all over, sorting out the good ones from the bad."

"You think of just about everything."

"Just about. Which reminds me, there's your unlikely assistant Miss Carmen Dravago. What kind of a name is that anyway? And don't bother to explain her. I'm sure you have a pat answer. But ultimately the police will pull it all together with a few well-placed questions. You think they won't notice she's conveniently disappeared? After all, her work is done. She was following Lugg, wasn't she? You figured things were getting too close for comfort, he knew too much and had to be silenced. Today was the day, except Bill got there first. But she was on the spot when she saw all the commotion. She waited for her chance and then, carpe diem."

"Miss Dravago is a very efficient assistant."

"Indeed she was. C'mon Gordon, this was the day, wasn't it?"

"It was a good day."

Kay twisted her mouth as though she'd eaten something bitter. "After Lugg was shot you and your helper just happened to be on the spot but far enough away for plausible deniability. By the way Miss Dravago's nimbleness of foot also explains how she got away the other day when she shot at me."

"You're very persistent, Kay. Maybe a little too persistent." Shellhammer pulled out a pistol. Kay felt a sharp chill shoot through her body and her skin tones became paler as she eyed the weapon.

"It's the same model that killed Lugg and fired the shots at you," Shellhammer said with cold precision. "Though not necessarily the same gun. I heard you'd been snooping around on your own. When you called me I surmised you were onto something and thus I might need a little more force."

"How perceptive of you."

"Your analysis is correct, mostly. Leena thought she could smooth-angle her way to the good life, playing both sides against the middle. She didn't figure on some people taking it kind of personal. It all added up to a fast curtain to the morgue. Tough break, but ours is a tough business."

"How do you plan to pull it off?"

"Pull it off?"

"Killing me?"

Shellhammer's face assumed a frown that was half way between thoughtful and quizzical. "I'll just say I was working late and that I heard shots and found your body. I'll mention something about hearing noises, gunfire, someone scurrying away, but that I didn't see anybody. Kind of tidy, don't you think?"

"And the gun?"

"I know this building. I can hide it in lots of places and get rid of it later."

"A good plan. But with one flaw."

"What's that?"

"I didn't come alone."

Shellhammer's blank look metamorphosed into a forced smile.

"You're bluffing," he said through laughter that was a little too silvery.

"No, Gordon, not bluffing. I'm a clever girl with more than my share of courage but I wouldn't be dumb enough to confront you at this hour without backup." She turned toward the office door and said in a louder voice, "Mr. Peele?"

A grim-lipped Dixon Peele walked into the office. He was followed by two armed security guards.

"Hello, Gordon," Peele said.

Shellhammer managed a clipped, "Am I supposed to say 'fancy meeting you here'?"

"Fancy or no, the police will be on the scene any minute. And another thing, in case you have any ideas, additional security guards are at all the exits." Peele delivered the words in a cold monotone.

Shellhammer took in a breath and his expression turned calm. "Well, Kay, you know I don't like to lose.

But I can see when I'm outflanked – for now. Here you are."

He tossed the gun in her direction but Peele reached over and caught it. Shellhammer clasped his hands and outstretched his arms. "Well, here I am, Dixon, all wrapped up. All that's lacking is the pink ribbons. And the handcuffs."

"That won't be necessary, Gordon. If you'll just come with us – "

Shellhammer methodically grabbed his hat from his desk, put it on and calmly walked out of the office with Peele and the guards.

CHAPTER 33 : AFTERMATH IN PARADISE

Kay and Powell sat in a secluded corner of the Paramount commissary. It was mid-morning and only a few customers lingered about on break.

Kay picked at her French fries. "Terrible food," she said.

"But the atmosphere is priceless."

"Glad you think so. Thanks for meeting me here."

"Don't mention it. I'm a coffee break guy from way back. But I've a few lingering questions."

"Fire away."

"How did you know it was Shellhammer who was behind it all?"

"I didn't. But it was the only explanation that fit. There were always rumors about payoffs but nothing concrete, no absolute proof. The scenario worked because Gordon had a reputation for fixing things. So I took a chance. Then there was the psychic, what she said."

"The psychic?"

"Yes. For all her bluff she got the envelopes filled with large bills right. Even more so the navy blues, the blue uniforms of the police department. Whether it was vibrations from the beyond or inside information, I didn't care. It all began to make sense."

A waitress showed up and dutifully refilled their cups of water while Kay lit a cigarette in the interval. She took a thoughtful puff then said, "Anyway I was able to finesse Gordon into showing his hand, and with witnesses around to boot."

"From how you describe it he talked a little too much. Word has it he's still talking, cooperating to a point, dangling just enough information. Claims it's all the studio's fault, that he's just a hapless pawn. You know, the usual sob story. Of course they say he was working on his own."

"I smell deal and cover-up in the works. But that's Gordon, playing all the angles."

"Well, direct evidence is pretty thin and he's got the best in town defending him."

"You mean Harrison Tumworth?"

"It'll be a miracle if the D.A. lands a glove on him. By the way, speaking of landing a glove, how did you know it was Lugg who iced the girl?"

"Again, process of elimination. It had to be someone from security if for no other reason than knowing how to get a car that conspicuous off the studio grounds. And he had to be tipped off, probably by Gordon, where and when the girl would leave that night. Anyway Lugg seemed a likely choice. A little too convenient, his being on the scene right after the police arrived. We caught a break with the used car guy's positive identification."

"Good points all. Joey Chicago sure came through for us."

"Yes. I relied a lot on his sleuthing, heavy handed as it was."

"Awfully decent of you to personally apologize to the used car fellow."

"It was the least I could do. Well, not quite the least. The little gratuity I slipped him helped ease the pain." She looked away for a moment while she drank a swig of water and pecked at her food. "What do your sources downtown say about Gordon's mystery woman Miss Dravago?"

"The cops don't have a thing and he's being mum. It's like she just vanished," Powell said.

"Well, people in that line of work don't carry business cards."

"How's your two friends Fallon and Archer? Behaving themselves?"

"Actually very good sports about it. Lt. Fallon gave me a bit of a tongue lashing about my confronting Gordon on my own, putting myself in danger and such. That and a few veiled threats about withholding evidence and consequences. The usual police intimidation. But he took my statement and that was that."

"Any ideas about these two being part of the dirty business?"

Kay's visage turned thoughtful and she said, "I don't think they are. I asked Lt. Fallon, carefully, about the payoffs, and he just said something like no comment. You know the old code of silence."

"I thought that attitude was reserved for the hard guys."

"Maybe so. I can't know for sure but they seem like straight arrows to me. The kind of fixing Gordon was involved in required high level intervention and I just don't see two beat detectives being players, except maybe incidentally. Call it a hunch but I see it as someone higher up the ladder. Whatever the truth is, the powers will take care of it internally, all very hush-hush. Some wrists will get slapped, but we'll never know the whole story."

"You're probably right."

"Fallon almost admitted as much to me. Anyhow, maybe someday, fifty years from now, an intrepid journalist will get it right. Perhaps something for my memoirs."

"Sounds like an idea. Oh, and congratulations on the near completion of *Trouble in Paradise*. I hear it's going to be something exceptional."

"We're all hopeful. How about you? Anything exciting on the horizon?"

Powell took in and let out a long breath. "A few things in the works. Word has it this Hammett fellow is working on a new detective story and it sounds like the main character is just made for me. He's calling it *The Slim Man* or something like that."

CHAPTER 34 : A RETURN

Finally a Saturday and time to relax. She lounged on her oversize living room sofa and listened to the sounds of *La Traviata* which wafted from the radio. She inhaled a cigarette puff and contemplated with pleasure the progress of *Trouble in Paradise*. Nearly finished it was. Even Miriam Hopkins was being relatively civil on the set.

The doorbell rang and she could hear Lupe talking to a man. Lupe entered the room and said, "Miss, a delivery man from the messenger company."

"A delivery man? Well, what does he have to deliver?"

"I don't know, ma'am. He says you need to sign for it."

"Oh, all right." She got up and walked to the door. The man standing outside was tall, blonde, athletic, and he wore a squeaky clean uniform.

"Miss Francis, an honor," he said with a shaky voice. He handed her a small parcel. "Special delivery.

Please sign here, and if I may bother you again, may I
have your autograph?" He flipped out a writing pad.

"But of course," Kay said as she obligingly signed
both with her usual florid handwriting.

"Thanks, thanks. My wife will be thrilled."

"Not at all. A pleasure." Kay flashed a warm smile
as she said the words.

He left and she wandered back into the living room.
She opened the packet and could hardly believe what
she saw: the rara avis itself. A handwritten note was also
enclosed.

My Dearest,

*Enclosed is the missing diary which has given you such worry.
If it's any consolation the diary has also been the basis for much
anguish on my part. Yes, my darling, I took the diary.*

*My real name, my professional name, is Franklin Meyerhoff.
You may have heard of me. For a time I had the distinction of
being on the FBI's most wanted list but more recently they've had
other challenges to deal with. Thus I've fallen off their roll of
honor. My professional vanity is bruised but a benefit is I've kept
a low profile and have managed to escape their attentions, as well
as that of the local authorities. Yes, my sweet, my work is that of a
professional confidence trickster and thus I possess all the
accompanying graces: manners, clothes, looks, even a veneer of
musicality to further entice you.*

*I showed up in your life to rob you, worse, to blackmail you.
But alas, I fell in love with you. Further alas, I cannot be in your
life any more as the people I work for are not so sentimental,
indeed not very nice sorts at all, and will be most displeased at my
failure to deliver the promised merchandise. Thus I must
disappear, at least for a time. I do so regret we couldn't have met
in happier circumstances. You are the true love of my life, and have*

been a most wonderful and engaging companion for this all too brief interlude.

By the way permit me to congratulate you on the successful resolution of the murder case. A brilliant bit of work on your part. One final thing: I've taken the liberty of one nostalgic indulgence, a token for my time and trouble. Specifically the pearl necklace from your drawer in the bedroom dressing stand. Out of regard for you, my dear, I chose not your most expensive necklace, but the more modest ornament. You know it, the one strewn with the small diamonds, the Tears of Desire I believe you called it. I hope you'll understand my need for this little memento and not carry sadness or bad feelings.

Yours always,
'René'

Kay read the last paragraph through steamed eyes, but managed a soft, "With the compliments of KF and company."

EPILOGUE

One month later …

In her back yard Kay indulged herself with a donut and martini as she read the first reviews of *Trouble in Paradise* in the morning papers. The more she read the more she floated in a sea of joy and disbelief. She'd gotten good notices before but never anything like this. They were all overflowing with praise, gushing and spewing like Victoria Falls on a hot, steamy afternoon. She scanned yet another positive article, this one from the *Portland Herald*:

TROUBLE IN PARADISE – DELIGHTFUL COMEDY OF MANNERS AT THE PALACE. "Steal, swindle, rob, but *if you treat her like a gentleman, I'll break your neck." Thus the delicious ambiguity of* Trouble in Paradise, *director Ernst Lubitsch's new comedy which just opened at the Palace.* Paradise *sparkles like a polished emerald with its Old World wit, brittle sophistication and sly innuendo. Mr. Lubitsch's direction is a reservoir of nuance, his customary polish and matchless style never more self-assured.*

Much credit is due to Sam Raphaelson's script which jumps off the screen with its clever repartee and urbane savoir-faire. But hors concours *must certainly go to the flawless casting, especially the principals Kay Francis, Herbert Marshall and Miriam Hopkins. The performances of Mr. Marshall and Miss Francis in particular are a model of smoldering passion cloaked in a veneer of aristocratic detachment. Mr. Marshall delivers his lines with his familiar mellifluous voice, his words sculpted like finely wrought crepe de chine. And Miss Francis is a wonder of delicacy and understatement. Like her wardrobe her character renders her emotions with the veiled transparency of a see-through négligée.*

Never mind that our story - a love triangle wrapped in a touch of larceny - has essentially no substance. For style is supreme in this production in which all is strewn together in a gossamer texture of angel dust floating in the clouds. Indeed while experiencing a movie this good we glimpse paradise for a moment. See it for yourself. You'll not be disappointed.

She hesitated, looked away and mused that this writer certainly had a way with the phrases. The words just rolled off his pen like — well, like …

She heard the faint tinkling of the phone in the house. It was Lupe's day off so she got up from the lounge chair, walked into the living room and answered it herself.

"Kay Francis speaking."

A few seconds later a familiar voice. "Kay, it's Nora. First, apologies for not doing a better job on helping your protégé's career. Just not enough time."

"Not a problem. He's, well, not exactly my protégé anymore."

"Oh, sorry."

"It's all right, really. Where are you?"

"Oh, I'm back in Los Angeles. What a whirlwind trip! Buenos Aires was simply divine. You just have to go there some day."

"Lovely. Glad to hear it was a good trip."

"Now, Kay, there's something I've got to talk to you about." Nora's tone had changed.

"Well, I'm listening."

"No, no. Not over the phone. That won't do."

"Why the mystery?"

"I can't go into it here. But let me say it's a matter of life and death, literally."

Kay knew Nora wasn't a kidder in these matters.

Nora continued: "And your specialized skills and knowledge … Oh, I just can't talk about it now. How about tomorrow, the Garden of Allah, the palm court. Lunch?"

"That sounds fine. See you then."

ACKNOWLEDGMENTS

Many individuals merit expressions of appreciation in the preparation and writing of this book. First and foremost huge thanks to Pat Coil, who proofed and edited the manuscript, in the process providing much insight with her matchless criticism. Also to Bev Johansen who read the first draft, proofed the final copy, and made constructive suggestions. Likewise thanks to Sharron Shipe, who proofed the final copy.

Several individuals examined cover designs and offered valuable feedback and suggestions: Sandy Bazinet, Gretchen Beaubier, Pat Coil, Scott Free, and Cathy Wright.

Specialized thanks is due to the writing groups for their encouragement and information, in particular Southwest Writers and the Albuquerque chapter of Sisters in Crime. Much appreciation also to my current blogging community for their support.

Numerous sources both print and online were consulted, but the below-mentioned two principal biographies of Kay Francis were especially useful.

And of course extraordinary thanks is due to Kay Francis, Herbert Marshall, Miriam Hopkins, Ernst Lubitsch, and all the other individuals connected with the creation of the film *Trouble in Paradise*, which served as a most inspiring and challenging backdrop for a murder mystery.

ABOUT THE HEROINE

Kay Francis was one of the most successful and best-known film actresses in the 1930s, but her star faded quickly in the latter part of the decade. Today she's largely unknown except to a coterie of film buffs, though happily this seems to be changing.

There's much readily available biographical material, all of which helped the writer in no small measure in constructing this admittedly fanciful tale. Principal among these is the Kay Francis Archives at Wesleyan University, which includes scrapbooks, correspondence and other memorabilia, but most important, her daily diaries from 1922 to 1953. Alas, the diaries are not available online, but they are extensively quoted in various sources, the most important being the two biographies [1], which provide a detailed look at her professional and personal life as well as insightful commentary on the films.

There are also numerous postings and fan pages on the Web and many pictures through sources like Google Images. Then there are the films themselves. Though some are available on DVD, much of her oeuvre remains to be released.

She achieved her greatest success in the early Thirties, when she frequently appeared in "women's pictures." Among her distinctions is being the first actress to portray Florence Nightingale in the sound era. By the mid 1930s she was one of the highest paid persons in the world, her salary at over $5,000 per week.

Her date of birth is still the subject of some uncertainty, the most frequent dates given being 1899 and 1905. She married five times, and sources suggest her last divorce took place around 1940. In the 1940s her career rapidly declined and she appeared in a few B pictures. After her last film in 1946 she toured in regional theater, one of her prominent roles being that of Julia in Somerset Maugham's *Theatre*. The last two decades of her life she lived as a semi-recluse in New York City.

With no living immediate family members upon her death in 1968, she left the bulk of her considerable estate to Seeing Eye, Inc., which trained guide dogs for the blind. After her death her body was immediately cremated, and her ashes scattered.

As much as she was a very public figure at the height of her career, Kay Francis today remains something of an enigma. She confided much to her diary, but ultimately was a very private person; she was known to be superstitious and had an interest in numerology, but otherwise little is known of her spiritual beliefs. Though she described herself as a Roosevelt Democrat, she offered few political opinions. Frugal with her money, she was nonetheless generous to friends. Even with all the scholarly and popular material available on her, it seems there is still much to be discovered about Kay Francis.

[1] Lynn Kear, *Kay Francis: A Passionate Life and Career*, McFarland, 2006; Scott O'Brien, *Kay Francis: I Can't Wait to be Forgotten: Her Life on Film & Stage*, BearManor Media, 2007.

ABOUT THE AUTHOR

B. C. Stone is the author of *Coda in Black*, *Murder at the Belmar*, and *Midnight in Valhalla*. *Peril in Paradise* is the third entry in the Kay Francis mystery series. He lives in Albuquerque, New Mexico. Prior to writing novels he worked as a librarian at the University of New Mexico. He maintains a blog on books and writing, *The Vagrant Mood* at: http://vagrantmoodwp.wordpress.com

Made in the USA
Lexington, KY
30 July 2019